DARKNESS ASCENDS IN MAGIC CITY

DARKNESS ASCENDS IN MAGIC CITY

MAGIC CITY CHRONICLES™ BOOK SEVEN

TR CAMERON MICHAEL ANDERLE MARTHA CARR

DISRUPTIVE IMAGINATION

This book is a work of fiction. All of the characters, organizations, and events portrayed in this novel are either products of the author's imagination or are used fictitiously. Sometimes both.

Copyright © 2021 LMBPN Publishing
Cover by Fantasy Book Design
Cover copyright © LMBPN Publishing
A Michael Anderle Production

LMBPN Publishing supports the right to free expression and the value of copyright. The purpose of copyright is to encourage writers and artists to produce the creative works that enrich our culture.

The distribution of this book without permission is a theft of the author's intellectual property. If you would like permission to use material from the book (other than for review purposes), please contact support@lmbpn.com. Thank you for your support of the author's rights.

LMBPN Publishing
PMB 196, 2540 South Maryland Pkwy
Las Vegas, NV 89109

Version 1.00 July, 2021
ebook ISBN: 978-1-64971-880-8
Print ISBN: 978-1-64971-881-5

The Oriceran Universe (and what happens within / characters / situations / worlds) are Copyright (c) 2017-21 by Martha Carr and LMBPN Publishing.

THE DARKNESS ASCENDS IN MAGIC CITY TEAM

Thanks to the JIT Readers

Larry Omans
Wendy L Bonell
Dave Hicks
James Dyer
John Ashmore
Dorothy Lloyd
Jeff Goode
Diane L. Smith

If I've missed anyone, please let me know!

Editor
Skyhunter Editing Team

DEDICATION

For those who seek wonder around every corner and in each turning page. Thank you choosing to share the adventure with me. And, as always, for Dylan and Laurel.

— *TR Cameron*

CHAPTER ONE

Ruby Achera crouched on the roof of a nondescript building a block away from the Magic City Strip. Light and noise spilled from the nearby casinos, interfering with her ability to survey the surrounding area properly. She complained, "I don't know why you had me start here."

Over the comm built into her magical mask, which displayed her face as a dragon to hide her true features, Demetrius laughed. "You're aware that you've been whining since the moment you got out there, right?"

"Easy for you to criticize, back there comfortable in your bedroom."

"As I recall, it was you who couldn't relax enough to hang out and who needed to get out and do things."

Ruby sighed. "Yeah, my life is full of dumb decisions. Let's stop this discussion right here, shall we? You're no kind of armchair therapist, and even if you were, I don't want to be analyzed by my boyfriend."

He laughed again. "Coward."

She managed a grin. "Sure, that's it."

The technologically advanced lenses that Kayleigh, the tech for Diana Sheen's agency, had installed highlighted a moving dot in her visual field an instant before Demetrius reported, "Inbound."

"Got it. South?"

"Yep, plan hasn't changed."

She turned and ran, calling up a force shield close to her body to protect her from any attacks by the drone. For now, she was counting mainly on evasion, and portioned another bit of magic into her muscles to increase her speed. When she reached the end of the building, a force blast propelled her up and over to the next.

Ruby hit and tumbled into a somersault, the heavy leather of her base layer protecting her from sharp edges on the gravel surface beneath her. She rolled up without losing substantial momentum and noted she could now hear the whine of the pursuing vehicle's propellers, which motivated her to shift into a jagged serpentine to discourage any attacks. "Any answer yet as to whether this thing is autonomous?"

Demetrius replied, "It's almost certainly driving itself, my analysis bot says. It could get taken over at any moment, of course."

The warning tone in his voice inspired another smile. *So nice that you're that protective after putting me out here in the crosshairs in the first place. Yeah, okay, I'm the one who decided to come out here, it's true.* "Like the agents in *The Matrix*. I get it."

She cut hard to the right and turned, abandoning her southward route for a westerly one. The yellow line in her eyepiece told her where Demetrius wanted her to go, and she laughed inwardly for a moment at the thought that she was no longer truly autonomous but was an extension of the infomancer's will. *Not going to mention that. He'd enjoy it way too much.*

Ruby leapt over another of the intervening streets that made up the grid layout of the southern part of the city. Fortunately, the roads were single lanes in each direction, this area not having to deal with all that much traffic. For all the attractiveness of the Strip and the tourist trade it inspired, Ely, Nevada, was still a fairly small town. *Nothing like Vegas, which is good. Can't compete one-on-one with the big dog, but we can certainly carve out our niche.* The eyepiece told her to swing south again, so she complied. Demetrius reported, "Uh-oh, the PDA has noticed you now."

He fed an image into her lenses that showed a schematic map from above, with two dots on it, one of which was outside her normal scanning range. "Are you sure it's them?"

His tone was annoyed. "Of course I am. Do you think I'd let you continue to be in danger if it wasn't the ones we were looking for?"

"You might, rabbit, you might." One of their favorite downtime activities was watching old Bugs Bunny cartoons, and they worked hard to insert as many references into their conversation as possible.

He laughed. "Rascally rabbit. Now we have a third. You should speed up so you hit the mark before they reach you."

"Easy for you to say, sitting on your ass in comfort," she grumbled as she put more magical power into her body. Her skill in that area had increased dramatically in recent weeks, more or less as a requirement for continued survival in the challenges she'd faced. *Who I am now and who I was when I returned to Magic City aren't particularly similar. That woman was hopeful she could scratch out a living while working toward her dream of becoming a professional technomancer. Now, I'm in a costume running across the rooftops, and, oh yeah, just one other little thing, I'm the new leader of the Mist Elves. I wish I could go back to punch former me in the mouth and order her to get the hell out of town.*

She laughed at herself. *Demetrius is right. I'm totally a whiner. Perhaps it's because I'm running rather than fighting.* "Okay, so tell me what you're getting that makes this all worthwhile."

"Well, I have vectors on each of the drones, and combined with the other sightings we've had and what I've gathered from the monitoring stations you all placed, I'm quite sure I can triangulate the drones' bases. Plus, once my bots get time to analyze the signal flow we're recording, we might be able to figure out where the PDA is controlling them from."

"You don't think it'll be at their launch point?"

"I wouldn't hazard a guess. If it were me, I'd put the two facilities in different locations. There's no reason they need to be near one another as long as they have powerful enough communication equipment. But then, I tend to be conservative about that kind of thing. If someone finds a trail to my stuff, I don't want them to find a trail to me, too."

She launched herself a little farther than intended, the momentum from her magically amped muscles combining with the force blast to send her skidding onto the next roof. She caught her balance by frantically windmilling her arms and dove to the side as the first drone flew in low and fired a stream of bullets at her. Ruby hit it with a force blast, the glancing blow enough to knock it out of line but not enough to take it down, and sped into a run again. "Says the guy working out of his bedroom. Also, that was a little close."

He replied, "Run faster, then. If anyone tried to trace my activities, they'd wind up looking somewhere far from here, believe me. If they got past that one, there'd be another false location and another, and after that, you guessed it, another."

"So what you're saying is you could do a total disappearing act on me at any second. That totally gives a girl relationship confidence."

Demetrius retorted, "That's not at all what I was saying. Does your brain really work like that?"

She felt a little silly admitting, "Well, more or less."

Her sister's voice joined the conversation. "Oh, please, D. You've been with her long enough to know that her brain doesn't work in *any* way. Or maybe you didn't notice. Like the pretty, vacant types, do you?"

He laughed. "I like Ruby's type, whatever that is."

Idryll, her shapeshifter companion, countered, "Oh, that's a safe answer. Clearly, you're afraid of her. Is she making you date her against your will? If so, you can tell us the truth. We'll rescue you."

Ruby sighed as she hurtled over the last street that separated her from her objective. The three dots were now all close enough that her local sensing had acquired them, and she did a jittering dance to avoid their attacks as she ran into position. "Okay, first, jealousy isn't a good look on either of you. Second, Morrigan, if you ever find someone willing to be your partner, you can feel free to have an opinion. Until then, remember, whatever makes me annoying is also in your genes."

Her sister inserted smoothly, "Oh, so you're saying Demetrius just likes you because of what's in your jeans?"

The infomancer burst out laughing, and Ruby growled, "I swear to heaven, I am going to set up a training date with Diana so I can beat your face in for the sheer pleasure of it."

Morrigan replied, "Anytime, anyplace. You probably won't want your boyfriend to see you humiliated, though." Her voice turned thoughtful. "Unless he's into that. Are you into that, D?"

Ruby stopped, spun, and cast a semicircular wall of force to separate herself from the drones with her left hand. With her right, she summoned a rectangle of metal about the size of her torso that they'd planted here earlier. "Social hour's over. Get your butts out here and help me fight these things."

CHAPTER TWO

Morrigan released the veil concealing her and Idryll atop the building they'd selected for their ambush on the drones. The dissipating magic revealed her, clad in her scarlet uniform with a hood covering her hair, and Idryll, in her natural fur and a magical mask. The shapeshifter wore an equipment belt low around her hips carrying some of Margrave's toys, but other than that was weaponless. *Well, aside from her claws, which could probably cut through steel.*

Morrigan's bow was extended and ready, and she reached back over her shoulder to pull an arrow from the quiver. Notches on the ends of each allowed her to differentiate between them, and she chose the new, heavy-duty lightning arrow. She wouldn't use it against a human unless keeping them alive wasn't a concern, which it usually was. Against a drone? *No mercy required.*

She fitted it to the bowstring on the run, then let it loose at the nearest unmanned craft, which had dipped lower to make a strafing pass at her sister. The projectile flew true and slammed into its nose. Electricity burst from the magic arrow, engulfing the drone and dropping it smoking to the roof. Morrigan laughed. "Man, I love lightning."

Idryll flashed by, growling, "Don't you dare destroy them all before I get a shot at one."

Morrigan was already searching for another arrow. Unfortunately, she'd only brought one of the special lightning versions due to her limited supply, so she selected explosive instead, reserving her regular lightning arrows in case of human targets. She drew the string backward and looked for a target. "Better move fast then, cat."

Idryll replied by cutting in between her and the nearest drone, which Morrigan found both annoying and satisfyingly trusting since Ruby's companion assumed she wouldn't wind up with an arrow in the back. The tiger-woman ran toward Ruby and shouted, "Give me a boost."

Ruby spun and cupped her hands. When the shapeshifter leapt into them, a powerful throw set her flying toward the nearest non-smoking attack drone. Idryll twisted in midair, and by the time she reached the craft, her claws were ready. They sliced through the mountings for two of the four turbofans in a single pass, and the vehicle careened out of control.

Ruby snarled, "Of course it's headed for the street." She threw up a wall of force and the drone slammed into it, rebounding to land on the building's roof.

It burst into flame, and Morrigan shifted the bow and arrow into one hand and used the other to cast ice over the fire before it could catch the building alight. "You two are completely reckless."

Ruby snorted. "Like you're one to talk, trigger-happy Barb."

Morrigan scowled at Ruby's use of the callsign Diana Sheen's people had given her. Somehow, when her sister said it, it always seemed like an insult. She muttered low curses and drew a bead on the third drone. Ruby shouted, "Mo, down." Without hesitation, she threw herself into a forward roll just in time to avoid a hail of bullets that punched into the roof behind her.

They'd chosen this particular building because it was currently unoccupied and slated to undergo a serious renovation. Demetrius had searched to find the location that would have the least impact on innocents while still serving their needs, and this had been the winner. The idea had been Ruby's, but they wouldn't have been able to pull it off without the infomancer's skills. *So, I'll give him all the credit.* She rolled up to her feet and growled, "What the hell? Where did that come from?"

Demetrius replied, "Additional drones. Must have flown in under a cloak of some kind or stayed undercover with active electronic countermeasures. I couldn't see them on cameras or signal sensors until they attacked. Probably operating autonomously with a limited instruction set."

Morrigan grinned. "Excellent. More robots to kill."

Ruby turned in a circle, taking stock of the new situation with her eyeballs as well. "Apparently, the Paranormal Defense Agency is all in today." A total of six drones were within a block of the building, and four more were less than a dozen seconds away.

Demetrius said, "We're lucky this one got out ahead of the others. If they'd all shown up at once, it could have been ugly."

"You think?" Ruby summoned the metal plate to her arm again, using a consistent stream of force magic to lock it in place as if she'd strapped it to the limb. The octopus tattoo chose that moment to squirm, sending nausea into her stomach as the artifact made yet another try to influence her decisions. *Knock it off, scumbag.*

She reached back and drew her sword, wishing she could cast through it. Sadly, there hadn't yet been an opportunity to engage in the training the Atlantean had offered. When her fingers met the hilt, the queasy feeling vanished as the twin entities inside Eidolon protected her mind.

Thanks, you two. Ruby positioned the shield in time to catch a barrage of bullets from the drone closest to her. She ran at it and jumped, slashing her sword at one of its fans, but it bounced into the air, clearly anticipating her move.

Demetrius advised, "Signals are flowing all over the place. They're probably remote piloted now."

Morrigan snarked, "Are you going to hit it, *Jewel*, or dance with it?"

Ruby spun and threw her sword at the one that had dodged her, sending it tumbling hilt over blade. The ungainly projectile passed right through a propeller, the sharp weapon shattering it and sending the vehicle out of control. Idryll had climbed onto one of the cooling units mounted on the roof and pounced on the drone, riding it down to the surface and stabbing her claws into and through it. Ruby reached out with her force magic and brought the falling sword back to her hand. "Less talking, more arrowing."

Morrigan replied, "So, is this a successful endeavor, Demetrius?" An arrow zipped from her bow to slam into another of the drones. It exploded on impact, sending the craft spiraling down to the street in pieces.

Ruby winced. *Hope there's no one down there. Of course, if anyone is stupid enough to stand nearby when they see this sort of thing going on, they kind of deserve what they get.*

Demetrius replied, "I have all the information I need. More won't help. Get yourselves out of there."

Ruby shook her head. "Not until we take these things out. Every one we destroy is one less they have to use. And most of these are the heavy-duty ones."

The infomancer had been monitoring aerial traffic throughout the city and had noticed smaller drones flying the same routes as those loaded down with weapons. He'd concluded that the PDA had chosen to supplement their information gathering with consumer models, which had drawn a curse from her at the time. *One would wish for less competent enemies.*

Idryll tackled her as a drone flew at her back, passing right through the space she'd occupied. The shapeshifter protected her from the fall with her body, which felt harder and stronger than normal, suggesting she'd done her partial shapeshift thing. Ruby said, "I doubt they're using anti-magic bullets."

Her companion released her and rose to her feet. "Finding out by getting shot would be pretty stupid, though, don't you think? Even for you."

Another drone went down, this one the victim of Morrigan's razor arrow, to judge by the fact that only the feathered end showed as the vehicle spiraled down. Her partners must have eliminated the rest because the one remaining visible drone suddenly flew up high, apparently happy to watch them instead of continuing the battle. Ruby said, "Okay, let's blow this popsicle stand." She reached inward for her magic and summoned a portal at the side of the roof to take them back to the bunker that was their secret base.

At least, that's what she *tried* to do. However, the rift failed to appear, and her access to her power suddenly fell away. She growled, "Anti-magic emitters," at the same moment Demetrius reported, "Enemies inbound." Ruby turned to see PDA agents in battle gear climb over the edges of the roof, wearing the anti-magic emitter backpacks that had become a normal part of their loadout in Magic City. "Dammit. Okay, remember, no killing. That includes accidentally knocking them off the roof, Idryll."

The tiger-woman replied, "It hurts that you would think such things of me. Also, that's a stupid rule. They chose to come up here. They deserve whatever comes to them."

"I don't think Alejo will see it that way."

Morrigan stepped up beside them. "Less talking, more fighting." She fired her grapnel and snagged one of the agents that had gained the roof, yanking forward so they stumbled and fell. Then she retracted the line.

Ruby said, "I'm serious, no killing. Once we get an opening to escape, we go."

Demetrius replied, "You'd better get a move on, then. There's a chopper inbound."

CHAPTER THREE

Ruby said, "What the hell do you mean, a chopper?"

Idryll ignored the conversation as she ran toward the edge of the roof, heading directly for the nearest enemy bringing their rifle into play. It was a bad situation, given that the building wasn't that big in the first place, and there seemed to be a lot of the enemy around. Fortunately, she didn't need additional magic beyond what nature had already provided, so their backpacks were irrelevant to her.

She reached the agent as the barrel came up, whipped out one clawed hand to slice through the strap holding the weapon, and yanked the gun away with the other, throwing it off the roof. The look of shock visible through the transparent faceplate was rewarding, and she resisted the urge to send him over the edge after it.

Instead, she kicked the man's legs out from underneath him and pushed into his fall, slamming him onto his back. She grabbed the helmet and wrenched it off, then dove aside as bullets *thwacked* into the surface near her. *Friendly fire is not my fault.* She ran in a serpentine for the cover of some nearby equipment, sliding around the corner to safety as rounds smacked into the object's metal skin. She said, "I'm not so great against bullets."

Ruby replied, "Yeah, this kind of sucks, no doubt about it. Demetrius, add a drone loaded with knockout gas to our to-do list."

He confirmed, "Got it. Of course, their helmets would stop that."

"Always with the negativity. Idryll, stay safe, look for targets of opportunity."

Morrigan offered, "Here, let me give you some."

Idryll stuck her head up over the lip of her cover and saw an arrow stab into the roof in the center of a cluster of agents who had moved a few feet away from the edge. They staggered and fell as if their bodies had forgotten how to stay balanced.

Ruby distracted the others on the roof, shooting at them from behind a piece of equipment, which allowed Idryll to sneak out and strip the fallen of their rifles. For good measure, she cut their backpacks from them and threw them off the side as well. She managed to take care of three of the five before someone noticed her and forced her to dive and roll back into cover to avoid the bullets. "That was fun. Let's do it again."

Morrigan replied, "That was my only sonic arrow. Now that you've got their helmets off, I can gas them, so at least those will be out of the fight."

Ruby said, "Okay, I'm going to do something stupid. Keep your eyes open, Idryll. You may get an opportunity."

She snorted. "You say that like it's different from what

you usually do." Nonetheless, she peered over the edge of her cover and readied herself to move.

Ruby sighed. "Not the time for insults, you know?" She glanced down at the dart gun encircling her right arm. *Five rounds. Gotta make them count. They're wearing vests, so the torso is a no-go. Plus, can't hit anyone who's too close to the sides. Gee, this is fun.*

She burst from hiding, firing her pistol into the air with her left hand as a distraction. She lined up the first enemy on the move and pressed the stud to fire the dart. It flew out and punched into the agent's arm. Her target wobbled, then fell, as the fast-acting drug rendered them unconscious.

She slid to avoid gunfire from the next, firing as quickly as she could bring her arm in line. That one went down with a dart to the leg. Her torso shouted in pain as bullets thudded into her vest from her left. She twisted and snapped out another dart, which lodged itself in her opponent's vest. *Damn it.* She fired the next, scoring the arm, and took a bullet in her arm before the agent fell.

Gritting her teeth, Ruby forced herself to stand and run for the nearest cover as quickly as she could. She launched her last dart on the way, not waiting to see if it scored before diving behind the small housing that protected the door leading down into the structure.

Morrigan asked, "Are you okay?"

Ruby replied, "Perforated, but still going. What's the situation?" The arrival of a helicopter overhead and six agents sliding down on lines answered the question effectively. She shouted, "Go," and ran toward the newcomers. Their only chance was to take them out while they were focused on the descent because six more rifles could easily turn the tide against them.

Morrigan said, "I'll knock out the chopper."

Ruby snarled, "No, it might crash. Alejo, remember?"

Her sister sighed. "Rules. I hate rules. Let's mix it up, then."

Morrigan hit the button to collapse her bow into its baton form and shoved it into the holster on her left leg at a run. She didn't draw her knives since her reflexes might cause her to launch a fatal strike rather than one that her opponent would survive. She counted seven more of the infernal emitters blocking them from their magic, the newcomers plus one other. "Idryll, see if you can get the backpack off that last one."

The shapeshifter replied, "On it."

Morrigan swept the feet out from under the nearest agent as they released the line, sending them crashing to the roof. She spun around the second, making sure the first couldn't shoot her from his prone position without hitting his companion and kicked that one in the back of the knee.

He went down to his knees, and she wrenched his helmet off and tapped him on the temple with her stun knuckles. They discharged with a loud *snap*, and the man crumpled. She abandoned him and moved for a third. He brought his rifle into line, but she slapped it down as he pulled the trigger.

His bulletproof vest thwarted an elbow smash into his solar plexus, but a follow-up hammer fist to the nerve junction in his leg caused him to go down on one knee. Again, Morrigan wrenched off his helmet and tapped his temple. *Two down.* Then bullets slammed into her back, and she pitched forward over the edge of the roof.

She couldn't catch her breath, but she managed to retain enough presence of mind to launch the grapnel attached to her right arm. The magnetic harpoon snagged the fire escape and snapped taut, swinging her to slam against the rusted metal a story down with a loud *clang*. She grabbed the railing, pulled herself over, and threw herself against the building's wall so that anyone peering over the edge from the top would have a difficult time spotting her.

Ruby shouted, "Morrigan, are you okay?"

When her lungs finally gathered enough breath to answer, she replied, "Yeah, I'll be back in a minute." She grabbed a healing potion, downed it, and gritted her teeth against the pain as broken ribs knitted themselves back together. *Just a couple of seconds, then I'll get moving. Promise.*

Idryll dashed out and caught the last remaining member of the original group looking the other way. She punched the agent in the left kidney, then in the other one. To their credit, they didn't crumple but instead whipped the rifle around in a clumsy strike at head-level. Idryll ducked under it and came up slashing, cutting the strap that secured the weapon.

She lashed out a hand and knocked the gun away, then deflected a flurry of punches and a kick from the agent. She threw a punch at his temple. He blocked, stepped in, and locked out her arm to throw her.

She performed a flip to reposition and negate his leverage, then seized his arm and used it to swing herself down at his legs. She pulled him down on top of her, grabbed his helmet, and ripped it off. He immediately slammed his forehead down at her face.

Idryll twisted away and took the blow on her ear, starting a ringing throughout her skull. *I've had about enough of this adventure.* She wrenched herself to the side, throwing him off her, and was on her feet by the time he regained his. He stepped back into a fighting stance and yanked a baton from his belt, snapping it out to full length.

Idryll shook her head and displayed her claws. "Really? You think that toy is going to help you?"

He didn't reply, just attacked with a rush and a downward angled strike at her neck. She flowed away to her right and slammed a knee into his stomach, but his body armor absorbed the impact. He snapped an elbow at the back of her head, and she dove forward into a somersault to avoid it, coming quickly to her feet.

Idryll waited until he committed to motion, then rushed forward, counting on her unexpected mass and strength to carry the exchange. She took a blow from the baton on her left arm, numbing it from the shoulder down, but rammed her body into her opponent hard enough to send him and his baton flying in different directions. He was on his hands and knees, shaking his head when she reached him.

She sliced the straps of his backpack with her claws, threw it over the side, and stomped down on his ankle to break it. He howled in pain. "Sorry, bud, but it's better than getting thrown off the roof or dying from brain damage if a punch hits a little too hard."

She headed for her partners at a run.

Ruby took out her first foe before he landed by grabbing him and yanking him off the rope, then ripping off his helmet and knocking him unconscious with the stun knuckles on her right hand. She delivered a sidekick to the next that thrust him into a third, then pursued both of them as they stumbled back.

One of them veered toward the edge, and she adjusted her path to snag him before he toppled over, pulling him onto her and throwing him over her head as she fell on her back. *Captain Kirk has nothing on me.* She rolled to the side as bullets struck the surface beside her and kept going right off the side of the building since it was either that or accept increased perforation.

She grabbed the edge as she rolled over and found her footing well enough to jump to the nearby fire escape. Morrigan grinned as she landed. "So, you fell off the roof, too?"

Ruby shook her head. "I heard you slam against this thing, so I knew it was here. I simply executed a timely strategic retreat."

Her sister replied with doubt in her tone, "Seemed a little less strategic and a little more frantic, from my perspective."

Ruby pounded up the stairs with Morrigan a couple of steps behind. When they reached the roof, they found Idryll finishing the last one by snapping his forearms so he couldn't hold a weapon. *Harsh, but undeniably effective. Need to add some zip ties to her equipment belt.*

Together, they removed the remaining backpacks and headed toward the building's edge to portal away out of view of the fallen. Ruby's paranoia over people looking through her portals and finding out her secrets had only increased over time.

As her sister created the portal, Ruby happened to look down and spot a figure in the alley below. He was looking up, watching her. She immediately recognized the Drow she'd met in the warehouse, the one who was behind the anti-human sentiments spreading through the city.

He tipped the wide-brimmed hat that hid his white hair to her and sauntered away. She considered going after him, but her appetite for adventure had been completely satisfied for the evening, especially since she hadn't found time to take a healing potion yet. *I really need to get some of Daphne's capsules made.*

She shook her head and followed her companions through the portal with a scowl. *PDA jerks. You're lucky we promised Alejo we wouldn't leave any bodies behind, or you'd find messing with us far more costly.* She considered the number of drones they'd destroyed and brightened. *Well, at least we hit you pretty hard in the pocketbook tonight. That's something.*

CHAPTER FOUR

Paul Andrews paced at the head of the conference table in the PDA's rented Ely bureau, expending effort to appear calm and measured as he took precisely calculated steps. Three in one direction, turn, three in the other. Or at least he *hoped* he looked calm. Anyone in his office who remained unruffled despite their recurring failures to take down the masked vigilantes haunting the city should probably be fired.

Charlotte Krenn continued speaking, bringing his attention back to the moment. "So, as you all know, one of our primary targets provided us the opportunity to test out new strategies yesterday. The good news is that the drones operated in every area exactly as we had hoped. The autonomous functionality got them there quickly, and our operators were able to seamlessly take control of two and employ them effectively in battle."

Andrews interrupted, "We need to increase that capability. Arrange for a couple more piloting stations to be installed. While using one station to pilot multiple drones is fine for simple surveillance, it's obviously not adequate for combat situations."

She nodded. "Will do, boss." After a pause, probably to see if he was going to say anything else, she continued, "They were aware that anti-magic bullets might be part of the crafts' armament, as they used magic to interpose physical barriers. Still, we should load them up with anti-magic rounds, anyway. All we need is one second of surprise to take one of them out. And, with additional piloted vehicles, we can bring them in from different directions simultaneously."

"How many did we lose?"

She grimaced. "Six heavy drones, and two of the consumer surveillance models."

He grunted. "Expensive research. But sometimes you gotta do what you gotta do, right?"

Murmurs of assent came from around the table, where everyone who worked in the office had assembled. It would be a long day for those on the second shift, but communication was vital, and in-person was always best. *Prevents them from misunderstanding exactly how serious this is.* "What about the troops we deployed?"

She shook her head. "That part was less successful, although the targets didn't kill any, and only three injured enough to warrant a trip to the hospital. Broken bones."

He scowled. "Well, I'll say this for the costumed freaks. They're careful not to get on the wrong side of a murder rap. Probably a smart choice. Why didn't we do better?"

Video of the entire operation was available from a drone that had stayed high to capture it. Andrews preferred to let his subordinates share their analysis before he watched the recording. He thought they saw it as a mark of trust that he wouldn't insist on seeing the video firsthand. While that was true, and he did trust them, he would eventually watch it anyway to ensure nothing slipped through. *Trust, but confirm.*

Charlotte replied, "Fighting on the roof was a serious limitation from the outset. It was a challenging deployment, especially given that they probably could've magicked the helicopter right out of the sky if they'd wanted to."

"It was a good choice on their part. Shows us we don't want to allow them to choose the battleground again, that's for sure."

His subordinate sipped from her water bottle before continuing. "I think the most important lesson learned on this one is that our people shouldn't engage at close range if we can help it."

Andrews let out a small laugh. "Unfortunately, snipers are contraindicated for this situation since our targets technically haven't committed a crime of sufficient magnitude." *Perhaps we should use them anyway. It seems like coloring inside the lines isn't going to get this done. Or at least not soon enough to make a difference. It would look pretty bad if another casino went down while we have boots on the ground in Magic City.*

He stopped his pacing, turned, and placed his palms flat on the table, leaning over and letting his gaze fall on everyone seated around him in turn. "Okay, here's what we'll do. You are going to work the phones and call your most reliable contacts, every one of them. I want you to beg, borrow, requisition, or steal replacement combat drones. Someone will have to talk to the techs and find out how many consumer models they need and arrange that, too."

Everyone nodded, and he looked up at his subordinate. "Charlotte, you get to handle acquiring a big shipment of anti-magic rounds. Might be worth reaching out to the military, as well as the government. They might be willing to let us sneak a little from the stockpile."

She grimaced. "That'll take some time, boss."

"Yeah, I know. So, you all better get to it. Go." His team filed out of the room, but he grabbed Charlotte by the arm before she could follow.

When the door closed, he said, "We're going to work on another angle as well. I want you to beat the weeds and see who the best available bounty hunters are at a price point we can accommodate. Then, have our infomancer break into the Ely PD systems and seed crimes and bounties on the three vigilantes, along with the descriptions we have."

Her eyes widened, but her face didn't otherwise express her surprise. "You sure, boss? Ethical line, there."

He grabbed the back of his chair and pulled it out, then gestured her to the one nearby. When she was seated, he said, "Okay, here's my logic. Tell me where you disagree. Base situation, we have multiple bad things going on in this town right now, and we're stretched thin on the ground." He held up a finger. "First, a casino went boom, and we still don't know who or why."

She lifted a hand slightly, and when he nodded permission, said, "Wasn't that Gabriel Sloane? If so, doesn't that close that case?"

He leaned back in his chair and laughed, steepling his

fingers in front of his chest. "The Ely PD thinks so, but it doesn't ring true to me. He wouldn't have been working alone, which implies partners, and even one partner means someone could still be pushing whatever agenda he was after."

"Trying to get an 'in' with the casino businesses?"

"As far as we know, sure. Since they're not allowing it, anyone who wants to accomplish that will have to do it by questionable methods." She nodded. He extended two fingers. "Second, we have the anti-human movement."

Charlotte replied, "Yeah, I didn't mention it during the briefing, but we've increased our surveillance in the south of the city to look for them, too. It's hard, though. Unlike the costumed group, we can't really do recognition scans with the drones unless you want a bunch of false positives from every magical in town."

"That is indeed a quandary. Keep working on it. Eventually, we're going to get faces, and when that happens, we can have the bots do their thing."

"Unless their faces are fake, like magical or something."

He shrugged. "In which case, we're no worse off than we are right now. But we need to keep more humans in the loop. Increase the people watching the drone feeds in real-time. They don't need to be on site. Nab some Academy students for that one, too."

She nodded. "Will do." It always impressed him that she never wrote anything down and yet seemed to have every bit of relevant information at hand the moment he needed it. It was one of the many reasons he planned to take her with him whenever the agency reassigned him. *Hopefully soon.*

With a sigh, he leaned forward again. "So, on to number three, a seeming war among the security companies in town. Could be that's overstating the fact, but we have two strong pieces of evidence that argue for it. The alleged gas leak explosion at Worldspan headquarters is the first. Add to that the attack at Invention, which seemed notably lacking in objective other than to mix it up. If that *was* the goal, we can only assume that Aces Security was the target."

"Are you saying Aces was behind the building blowing up?"

He nodded. "That's my working hypothesis, as bizarre as it sounds. I mean, I don't see an obvious reason, and when you hear about corporate warfare, it's normally more of the backroom espionage kind of thing."

He shook his head. "Everything else is weird here in Magic City so I wouldn't put it past them. The real question, in my eyes, is whether there's someone behind them. If it's only them protecting turf, it seems pretty expensive. One would think the companies' primary concern is profit, rather than position."

She was silent for several seconds, then asked, "Do you think they're in with the vigilantes? Aces, I mean?"

He shrugged. "Doesn't seem like it, but who knows, maybe the costumes came to the gnome casino to intervene on the side of their allies. There's the fourth issue. Everyone thinks it's great when local citizens fight crime, but no one considers the fact that they're not following rules, and no checks and balances are in place to keep them from doing pretty much anything they want."

He recognized the same words could also describe him

at the moment, but he had risen through a system designed to weed out psychopaths and people who would misuse power. He couldn't say the same of the vigilantes.

Unless they're law enforcement, freelancing. That would explain a lot of their information. "You know, it just occurred to me that maybe we should review the rosters of police, sheriff, state police around here. See if any of them are magicals, for a start."

Charlotte nodded. "I agree. It does seem like they have a lot of inside knowledge and the sort of skills that would fit." She looked slightly uncomfortable.

"You still think this is an overstep?"

She lifted a hand and rocked it back and forth. "Might be. Might not be. I don't really have a guess as to where that line is."

He nodded and rose, and she copied his motion. "I always appreciate your counterarguments. Keep them coming. But right now, my position is that we must stop these vigilantes and the anti-human gang that's probably in league with them. So, I'm still convinced this is one of those moments where the ends justify out-of-the-ordinary means."

She nodded. "Then I'll get on the phone and let the local freelancers know it's hunting season for vigilantes in Magic City."

CHAPTER FIVE

Dieneth walked into the gourmet restaurant that was the primary draw of the Atlantean casino. *Well, other than the gambling, but that doesn't interest me at all. Money isn't an interesting stake anymore.* It was a strange place to be meeting his date, but she had explained it was important for her to visibly frequent all the casinos equally, as she was now the head of the Council.

He thoroughly understood the need to make an impression. That was more or less his whole purpose in Magic City nowadays. It was certainly a lot more fun than his previous gig as a dealer at Darkest Night, so low on the totem pole that the owner didn't realize that the man across the table had once worked for her.

He'd dressed for the occasion in a black suit, shining ebony shoes with a bit more heel than was particularly stylish, and a crisp, dark blue shirt underneath. In place of a tie, he wore a stylized wolf-head pin at his throat. Although it wasn't her casino, Elnyier had managed to secure a table in an out-of-the-way nook, and she nodded a greeting as he sat across from her. He asked, "Been waiting long?"

She gave him a small smile. "No, I just finished hobnobbing with the owners. They're an excitable bunch, to judge by how much effort they're putting into impressing me."

He laughed. "Well, that's kind of why you took the gig, right? What's old Maldren doing now, anyway?"

"He doesn't have any business interest in town, aside from a small percentage of ownership in the two Mist Elf casinos. So, he's spending some time on Oriceran, most likely licking his wounds and wondering where he went wrong."

Dieneth grinned, showing her his teeth. "You like that, don't you?"

Elnyier lifted an eyebrow. "How could you think such a thing?"

"Because I know you."

She brought her napkin up to pat her lips, probably to hide a smile. "I'll have you know I am only a member of the Council to serve my constituents. I have no ulterior motives whatsoever."

He laughed loud enough that a couple of people at nearby tables looked over at him. "Please. You're Drow. The only ones among us who have no ulterior motives are those who are already dead. Even then, you can't really be certain they're not up to something."

Elnyier dropped the napkin back to her lap, revealing her smile. "Of course, you're right. Yes, I do like that Maldren is out of the picture for the moment. Had he stayed, he could've proved a nuisance."

A bowl of soup appeared in front of each of them,

delivered by an Atlantean waiter who bustled away without a word. She said, "I've already ordered for both of us."

"Bold."

Elnyier shrugged. "That's what happens when you're late."

Dieneth chuckled. "Technically, I walked in the door exactly on time."

"Which means you were late."

He lifted the spoon and tasted the soup, an interesting seafood chowder in a tangy, spicy broth. "Oh, so you're one of those people, huh?"

"Of course. Early is on time." She waved her hand, and the world around them quieted. "So, we have a little privacy. How are your plans coming along?"

"Same as ever, seeking the tipping point that puts the humans in their proper place."

"I'll be using my position on the Council to do a lot of the same work you've been doing. The others don't have the stomach for a fight. That became clear during the whole Sloane incident when they essentially rolled over and hid in their shells.

"That gives me an opportunity. As things get more stressful on the surface, and the chaos builds, they'll be more likely to listen to offers for a buyout, or, worst case, to leave their businesses with younger, more resilient family members."

A frown turned down the corners of his lips, which he'd polished with some sort of strange sandy lotion he didn't fully understand in preparation for the date. *I should never have walked into Sephora alone. They can sense fear.* "I see where the former helps you. How does shifting ownership work to your benefit?"

Elnyier grinned. "Younger people are *much* easier to manipulate. You, for instance. A little shake, a little shimmy, and I have you eating out of my hand."

Dieneth laughed. "Well, I wouldn't put it quite that far. You're not that much older than me. But I can see where your statement is true, generally speaking." He paused as the waiter exchanged empty soup bowls for filled salad bowls, chopped vegetables with shrimp and salmon. "However, I doubt you're immune to my appeal."

She laughed. "Far from. You are an excellent partner, both in and out of the bedroom. Plus, you're pretty, which makes me look better out in public."

He shook his head but couldn't smother his smile. "You never turn off, do you?"

"Never. In fact, I'm not sure if you noticed, but the dwarf in the corner is one of Underground's owners' children.

He managed not to glance over. "Always on stage, I get it. I'm glad my people and I have been able to be of service toward your goals. Fortunately, after our initial statement, we haven't had to injure anyone seriously or kill to get our point across."

Elnyier nodded, set down her fork, and stared into his eyes. "It's time for that to change."

He'd expected such a thing would come from her, eventually. Whatever else he might be, he also was the leader of a group of muscle, and people usually employed muscle for a very limited array of purposes. "Do you have suggested targets?"

"I do. Would you like to guess?"

Dieneth laughed. "Okay, I'll take a shot. Um, you want us to go after the humans who have set up their little residential community outside the city limits."

She shook her head. "Boring. They're only low-cost labor at this point. Certainly, if they should become a threat, they'll be easy to deal with. No, I was thinking of bigger prey. Specifically, the Paranormal Defense Agency."

He considered the fact that he didn't choke on his food to be a major accomplishment. He set down his fork and chewed, then swallowed carefully. The waiter reappeared to whisk away their salads and replace them with a pasta dish, again heavy on the spice and the seafood. *Well, I guess that makes sense in an Atlantean casino. They probably just ask the fish to jump into the nets, and they comply willingly.* Finally, he replied, "That's rather bold, as well."

Elnyier nodded. "This is not the time or the place for half measures. My thought is that the Agents might overreact in very useful ways. The more they lock things down, the more upset the Council gets."

"And the more upset the Council gets, the more likely they'll turn to a strong leader and do as she suggests." His stunning partner inclined her head in affirmation. "Damn, woman, I like the way you think."

After dinner and dessert, he'd expected they'd go back to her place or his place to finish the evening in a more active fashion. Instead, she took him into Darkest Night casino. It was entirely familiar, unchanged from when he had worked there before.

The sky resembled a field of stars, and the gaming tables were all in black, deep scarlets, and dark blues. Embedded against the ebon expanse above, barely visible enough to be sensed rather than seen, rested a variety of images to inspire fear: demons' faces, spiders, and many, many other creatures often found in nightmares. They distracted even the most hardened and unimaginative person, which generally caused them to play worse and increased the casino's profits.

Elnyier led him to the upstairs offices, then took him to an elevator in the back of the hallway that connected the owners' suites. It opened at the touch of her fingers on a pad outside, revealing a narrow car with only enough room for four. They stepped in, shoulders touching, and she placed her hand on a matching screen on the inside.

The door swished closed, and the elevator started to descend. He quipped, "Make-out session in an elevator, huh? Well, I won't resist. It's a little weird, given the quality of your lodgings, but it's my sole desire to make you happy."

She let out a soft snort. "If that was my goal, I'd have you on one of my sisters' desks, just for the amusement it would give me later. No, we are about bigger things tonight."

The doors opened to reveal a small chamber, about ten feet by ten. Guarding a door on the opposite side were a pair of Drow in traditional battle gear, light armor with reinforced portions to cover essential spots. He followed Elnyier forward and only then noticed two more Drow stood in the corners on the same side as the elevator, with pistol crossbows aimed at him. He had zero doubt that they held poisoned bolts and not to render a target unconscious.

His companion strode to the left wall, where another hand plate waited. Her touch caused a small panel to pop free, and she retrieved a silver bracelet, about as wide as his thumb was long, etched with black sigils. She pulled it apart at the hinge as she approached him. "It's time for us to formalize this arrangement."

He nodded solemnly. "You're asking me to marry you? Of course, I accept. I'll need a stake in the casino and my own office. Is hitting on your sisters on the table?"

Soft laughter accompanied her head shake. "You are hilarious. Truly." She turned serious. "Swear now that you will be trustworthy and dependable. That you will never hear a word against me that goes unchallenged. That you will defend me with your life. That you will kill yourself, rather than turn traitor."

He nodded, recognizing the importance of her words and the significance of the bracelet she held. "I so promise. I shall remain faithful to the end of my life, or until the shared decision to free me from my vow." He pulled back his sleeve enough that she could slide the cuff over his wrist. When the two ends touched, the bracelet writhed momentarily and resolved into a solid band of metal, completely unremovable. It felt disconcertingly like the thing had chewed on him a little as it closed.

She smiled, a genuine one he'd seen only a few times before. "This object lets me know where you are. It can also," she paused as if searching for the right word, "*dissuade* you from acting against me, should that become necessary."

He nodded. "I've heard of such things and accept it willingly." He lifted an eyebrow. "You will properly reward my agreement in this matter, I presume."

With a laugh, she stepped forward and kissed him hard, pulling his face into hers. "Have no worries. Spoils galore await us both." The guards opened the door, and she led him through.

A portal rippled in the chamber. Elnyier explained, "This is permanent, self-sustaining by magic from the opposite side. It connects this place with my family's true home on Oriceran. My ancestors came through here and somehow rigged it to never close. Come on in, let me show you around."

CHAPTER SIX

Ruby scraped her knuckles along a sharp edge on the tiny drone that was part of her field gear. She dropped the screwdriver and muttered curses under her breath, then sucked on the knuckle, tasting the metallic tang of blood. *People are shooting at me all the time, but when it comes right down to it, I'll probably die of tetanus or something from an experiment gone wrong.* She shook her head and tried setting the panel properly in place again.

Magic happened nearby, hitting her senses like a gentle caress. It could only be one of her allies arriving. She rose, stretched, and ambled out into the main room. Idryll lay on the large chaise lounge they'd gotten for her, curled up like a cat despite being in her humanoid form. Ruby shook her head. "You are such a slacker."

The tiger-woman opened her eyes and gazed disdainfully at her. "I'm conserving my energy for when it's needed next."

"Ah. They say domesticated cats sleep twenty hours a day. Looks to me like you're trying to break the record."

"Jealous."

She sighed. "Guilty as charged. I could use a nap."

A sound from the side heralded the door to the receiving room opening. Her mentor, Phineas Margrave the Fourth emerged with a duffel bag in one hand and a small butcher paper-wrapped packet in the other. He grinned. "I see the kitty is resting again."

Ruby laughed, and Idryll replied, "You're jealous too."

He nodded, and his impressive brown handlebar mustache bounced. "I'll admit to that. Sleep is something I can never get enough of. Here, I brought you a present." He threw the smaller of the two objects to her.

Her companion straightened in time to catch it and immediately ripped it open. Inside was smoked salmon, one of her current favorite foods. The shapeshifter grinned. "Thank you. I consider the fact that Ruby didn't introduce me to this for so long to be an act of pure evil."

Margrave nodded, looking serious. "As do I. It's a wonder that you can even continue to be friends with her."

Around a bite of salmon, Idryll replied, "I'm just the bigger person, I guess."

Ruby rolled her eyes. "How about we get some work done for a change?" She headed into the workshop, and Margrave followed, laughing.

Once they were inside, she took her seat. He put his bag on the table, unzipped it, and proceeded to take out a box of tools, various components, and several smaller bags. He tossed the duffel to the side and sat. "So, what are we working on today?"

"First, let me show you my most recent success." Ruby rose again and walked over to a cabinet, opened it, and withdrew a large drone. "Hold this up." She handed it over. Margrave complied, and she used the controller to start the engine and to activate the bottom door. With a tinkling of metal, a couple of dozen caltrops fell out, cleanly separating as they dropped.

"Excellent. How'd you solve the clumping problem?"

"Put in a tube to redirect some of the airflow from the propeller through the storage compartment. It pushes them apart nicely." She took it back from him.

"Innovative. That might work for your other vision for it, too."

Ruby nodded as she stored it in the cabinet and kicked the caltrops off to the side. *I'll make Idryll clean them up later. That can be her work for the day. Give her something to complain about for a week or so.* "Yeah, I think ejecting them out the back with the stream of air should prove effective. It would require a pretty major redesign since the duct would have to go right down the middle rather than only through one side of the thing. But it has promise."

She sat again. "Okay, what I need from you is some help with locator tags and signal jammers. Plus, I've almost figured out the payload compartment for the tiny drone," she gestured at the small device on the table that had bloodied her finger, "but haven't quite gotten it working. I have the hardware in, but I can't figure out the weight."

He nodded. "Sounds like something I can help with. For the locator tags, I presume you want to use them on people, drones, cars, whatever?"

"Yeah. And they have to be small enough that people won't notice them."

"Magnetic?"

Ruby shrugged. "Some, sure. But we'll want versions with an adhesive, as well. In case we need to plant them on someone's clothes or on one of the plastic drones the damn PDA is using."

Margrave's expression turned serious. "I heard about your adventure with the Agency's drones. What did you do to tick them off?"

"My existence is enough, it appears. Although I don't think they like Morrigan or Idryll, either, so it's more of an anti-magical-vigilante sort of dislike than something personal."

From the other room, Idryll yelled, "I wouldn't be too sure about that. You're the only one who was in his bedroom."

Margrave lifted an eyebrow, and Ruby rolled her eyes. "On his windowsill, technically speaking. I guess one of my legs was indeed in the bedroom. I thought he might want to have an actual conversation. Turned out, not so much."

He shrugged. "Not a shock, I guess. Okay, the locator tags should be easy. I have the tech and some generic mounts in the toolbox, both adhesive and magnetic. A disc, you're thinking?"

Ruby nodded. "Yeah, maximum surface for the size."

He pulled out his notebook and jotted a few things down. "I can prototype that today, not a problem. On to the next thing. What sort of signals are you trying to jam?"

She frowned. They were entering an area of technology she wasn't strong on. The basics of how electronic communication worked were part of her degree, but she'd always relied on existing technologies rather than innovating her own. "I guess I don't really know the answer to that. Basically, I want to be able to use my equipment and interfere with others using theirs. That includes everything, drones, cell phones, encrypted comms, whatever."

"That'll be a little tougher. Probably the best plan is to get an off-the-shelf unit and refine it to a size you can carry. If we change the software to ignore the exact frequencies you use for your drones and comms, we'll at least be part of the way there. I'd have to do some research to target other frequencies specifically, though. Blanketing them all is a waste of power if we can figure out which ones are most likely to be used."

She nodded. "We can't disregard the possibility that they'll use an unexpected one. Maybe two modes?"

"Sure. It's just adding a switch, basically. Probably," Margrave corrected with a head shake. "This feels like one of those projects where you think you have it under control and it all goes sideways."

Idryll shouted, "That's the story of Ruby's life."

Ruby called back, "Hey, it's been a while since you took a nap. Almost ten whole minutes. Maybe you should get to it." She exchanged smiles with Margrave.

He said, "Let's get to work." They both picked up equipment and started applying tools to it. As they worked, they talked about small things, catching up on recent events. When she finished telling him the full story of the battle with the PDA, his expression was uncommonly concerned. "They really do have a bee in their bonnet about you."

She scowled. "They suck."

He laughed. "Apparently, that bee stings in both directions."

"That would make it a wasp, I suppose. But yeah,

they're a major problem, even more than most people think."

"Why is that? Other than the surveillance state they're trying to bring into being in Ely."

"We've got this rogue Drow whipping up the people in town, claiming that humans are repressing magicals. And here comes the PDA, acting in a way that exactly illustrates what he's saying. They're custom-made for each other. I can't imagine Andrews is in bed with that chaotic bastard, but on the surface, it sure looks as if both are rowing in the same direction."

"Not a pretty picture. Who are you going to deal with first?"

Ruby sighed. "That's the problem. Right now, we're very much reacting because we don't have the information or the clarity to choose a direction. So, I guess whichever one pops their head up next. The good news is that Demetrius has narrowed down the locations of the PDA bases in town. Maybe, if we're lucky, he can manage the same thing for the Drow and his group. I'm sure they're in a warehouse somewhere, but there are a lot of those about."

Margrave set down his tools and grabbed a bag that had been sitting next to him. "Then I guess you'll want these." He reached inside and handed over a bunch of patches with capsules mounted on them.

She recognized them immediately. "Daphne's work?"

He nodded. "With an assist from yours truly, of course. The healing potions are no different than normal, but the energy ones are the kickier versions she created. She's damn good at what she does. I took one the other day and forgot to sleep. Was up for forty-eight hours straight. Got a ton of work done, though."

She laughed. "Perfect." There were enough for her, Morrigan, and even Idryll, although how they'd stick one to her fur was an open question. *Maybe we can shave patches for them. Somehow I don't think she'd be in favor of that.* The image made her laugh, and she shook her head. "This is fantastic, thank you."

His hand disappeared into the bag again. "And, before you ask, I'm almost there on your dart reloads. I made the case, then I thought about it and realized that if I can spring-load them, they'll be easier to remove. So, I'll need a few more days."

She nodded. "Appreciate it."

He grinned. "Finally, take this." He withdrew a small featureless black box from his bag and slid across the table. "I managed to shrink down the locator tracker even more. Right now, it'll find all the people you've put implants in and interface with the tech in your mask. Once I get these other locators made, we can tweak the software to detect those, too."

Ruby grinned. "It's like Christmas up in here. You know what I'm going to ask for next, right?"

He sighed. "I imagine it'll be about the most difficult thing you can think of, so, a deployment system for the locators? To put them in drones, or a gun, or something equally challenging?"

She laughed. "You know me too well. Got it in one. You're brilliant, so that should take you what, a day and a half, maybe?" Her laughter continued as he stuck out his tongue at her with a look of exasperation.

"You know, I do have things to do for paying clients."

"Yeah, but this is way more fun."

Margrave rolled his eyes. "Your idea of fun is a little crazy, Ruby."

From the other room, Idryll shouted, "That pretty much describes Ruby's life. She's crazy. What happens around her is crazy. It's all just a big ball of insanity."

Ruby called, "Especially those I choose to hang out with."

He put his palm on his chest. "Present company excluded, of course."

She shook her head. "Not a bit, old man. Where do you think I get my abundant level of lunacy from?"

CHAPTER SEVEN

Grinding Axes was as busy as she'd ever seen it. Magicals of every shape and size filled the bar, and she nodded toward a couple in the corner. "Even Kilomea tonight."

Demetrius, looking dapper in black jeans and an untucked blue dress shirt, replied, "Oh, I met those two a while back. They're vacationing here from Oriceran, seeing what Magic City is all about."

"And they found the Axes? We're a little off the beaten tourist path."

He laughed. "There are tourists, and there are *tourists*. They aren't the casino-going kind. They're the learning about Earth kind. And I can't think of a better place to see magicals coexisting happily than here."

From behind the bar, Domick yelled, "Hey, strangers. Get over here." They obeyed and exchanged quick hugs with each of the dwarven bartenders before they returned to serving their customers.

Demetrius said, "I'll grab us drinks. You find the others." Ruby nodded. It wasn't that big a place, and she knew where to look. One of her roommates had thrown down a challenge at darts, and honor demanded a bout. Sure enough, Shiannor the elf, Daphne the witch, and Liam the dwarf were already near the dartboard, chatting and drinking while making practice throws.

They exchanged more hugs as Ruby arrived, and Shiannor commented, "You know, you'd think we'd encounter each other more often, given that we live in the same place."

Ruby shrugged. "It's a real busy life I lead. But fortunately, it's also completely unrewarding." The others laughed, and she slapped Shia on the arm. "Quit whining. You're the least social of any of us. I'm surprised to see you out."

Liam said, "He has his eye on someone who hangs out here. She hasn't arrived yet, though."

Daphne joined her in making the appropriate "Wooo" sounds, and the elf's skin colored a little. She asked sweetly, "Do you think it's warm in here, Shia?"

He scowled, muttered, "It's my turn to throw," and stepped away.

Ruby laughed and whispered, "Coward," knowing his sensitive ears would pick it up.

Daphne said, "I'm so glad you could come out."

Liam replied quickly, "Oh, it's no problem. I wouldn't miss the chance to hang with you."

The witch smacked him on the chest with the back of her hand. "Shut up, you. I'm talking to Ruby, and you know it."

He grinned. "Daphne's very abusive, now that she's a fancy business owner."

The other woman beamed. "Speaking of which, here, I have something for each of you." She reached into the overly large purse on the table beside her and pulled out a bunch of pins. Each displayed a stylized bright blue flask with a lightning bolt shooting through it. The background of the pin was an angled "D."

Ruby snorted. "Subtle."

Daphne offered her a theatrical scowl. "This, coming from someone whose family owns a casino, which is the very opposite of subtlety in every way. Besides, your people helped me create it."

Ruby laughed. "Exactly. Like I said."

Liam shrugged. "I don't know much about branding, but it looks good to me." He pinned it onto the black vest he wore over a white shirt. "Am I beautiful?"

Daphne giggled. "You're always beautiful." Ruby rolled her eyes. The two had always flirted, but of late, Daphne's soaring confidence had also led to increased intensity in her wordplay with the dwarf. *I wish they'd get a room. Wait, I guess I wish they'd get a hotel room, so I wouldn't have to hear them.*

Demetrius arrived. "Did I hear something about beautiful? You're talking about me while I'm not here. That's totally rude."

Ruby resisted the urge to give him a good shoulder-check since he was holding their drinks. She took a pint of beer from his hand and tasted it. "Good. From the abbey?"

He nodded. "Special keg. Brand new. Doesn't even have a name."

She sipped again and detected cinnamon, as well as some other thing she could recognize. As always, it was delicious. She shook her head. "Abbott Thomas is wasted as a religious person. He should be a full-time brewmaster."

Daphne said, "Maybe Spirits should become the craft beer source for Magic City. Open a restaurant carrying only the abby's brews."

Ruby blinked in surprise at the fact that such a brilliant concept had never occurred to her. "I'm definitely going to talk to my father about that. Genius-level idea. Your brain is firing on all cylinders, isn't it?"

Demetrius shook his head. "Daphne, you shouldn't show off like that in front of Ruby. You'll make her feel bad about her own, shall we say, less impressive brainpower." This time she did slam her shoulder into his, causing his beer to slosh onto his hand. He held it out. "It would be a shame to let even a single drop go to waste, wouldn't it? Want to lick it off?"

She smiled sweetly. "Want to be coiled up on the floor in immense pain while I finish the rest of your drink for you?"

He pulled his hand away as if he'd touched a live electrical wire. "I'll take that as a no. An emphatic one."

Laughter rewarded his words. As Shiannor rejoined them, Liam said, "Okay, let's take a minute for the reason we're here. To Daphne, may your success continue until you rule the world."

Everyone laughed, tapped their glasses together, and drank. They made a couple more playful toasts. Then the darts game began in earnest. The first round was Shiannor versus Demetrius. Ruby was the odd person out as Liam and Daphne talked with their heads close together, brows almost touching, clearly continuing their intense flirting.

Ruby finished her drink and headed to the bar for a refill. Jastrum, Domick's twin brother, came over. "The same?"

She nodded. "So, do you know Abbott Thomas?"

He laughed as he pulled the handle on the keg. "Every decent bar in Magic City makes a point of knowing Abbott Thomas. I swear he's figured out how to use magic for brewing."

She frowned. "He's human."

The dwarf delivered her drink and lifted an eyebrow. "Is he? Or is he a wizard in disguise?" He said the last as if sharing a secret, and she laughed.

"Conspiracy theories. I'm down. What else do you know? What other things do you think are going on?"

He spun out some well-rehearsed tales of Area Fifty-One UFO sightings, and she chuckled and nodded at the appropriate places while her body relaxed and her eyes idly scanned the crowd. She stiffened when she saw a familiar face in the corner, sitting alone with an empty glass in front of him. She tilted her head in his direction. "Does he come in here often?"

The bartender replied, "Yep, regular customer. Always alone, though. Has good taste in beer."

The decision was impulsive, but she didn't second-guess it. "Pull me another one, will you?" She took both glasses over to the table, set one in front of him, and sat on the opposite side. "Evening, Councilman."

Grentham snorted at her with a scowl. "That title

might've meant something once. Not so much these days. What is this?" He gestured at the drink.

She shrugged. "Whatever you want it to be. Gift from a stranger, attempt to lower your guard so you'll spill all your secrets, peace offering, or maybe just one of those gift horses you shouldn't look in the mouth."

He snorted again but took the drink and sipped it. "So, what does Ruby Achera, the allegedly human daughter of a prissy Mist Elf family, want with me? There are rumors out there, you know, that you're really half-human and not necessarily living with your birth parents."

She laughed. "First, maybe don't try to provoke me by insulting my family. I've heard it all before, and frankly, the jokes we make about ourselves are far more vicious.

"Second, I'm not sure. I've seen you around. I know you own a security company in town, and I know that someone attacked Invention while your people were guarding it. Seems like something all the casino owners should be concerned about. Do you have any details about it that I don't?"

He shook his head and mumbled, "Nope. Seems random. No idea why whoever it was chose to hit that casino in particular."

He was a terrible liar, but she didn't try to call him on it. Instead, she asked, "What's your beef with the Council? And to be fully honest, I'm not a big fan anymore, either. I thought Maldren had a pretty good handle on it. Elnyier, well, I don't think that's an increase in stability, let's just say."

He laughed and leaned back. "She's a total wench, but she's awful good at what she does."

"Which is?"

"Making deals. Wielding influence. Knowing when to use sugar and when to use a stiletto."

"So it's safe to say you didn't vote for her?"

He shrugged. "I wasn't confident in Maldren, either. She's right that he saw us through the time of building up Magic City, but she's also correct that he's not the person for the job at this moment. Of course, she waited until she had all the dominos perfectly aligned before she made her move, so there was no way to block her."

Ruby nodded and took a long draw on her drink. "My father said the same thing, that she doubtless had the votes already in hand."

Grentham grunted. "I would've voted for your father. We don't agree on everything, but he's got some ethics about him the others lack."

She lifted an eyebrow. "Are you the conscience of the Council, then?"

He laughed, and for the first time in their conversation, it sounded real. "Oh, *hell* no. Rules are made to be broken, more or less. As long as I'm not hurting anyone who's not in the game, not too many things are off-limits. But I'm not sure Elnyier shares even that basic level of concern with right and wrong."

She nodded. "Nor does the PDA, right?"

He scowled, the fiercest look she'd seen from him. "Those bastards are so far past the line they can't even see it anymore." He blew out a breath. "We should probably stop this conversation now. I'm starting to get angry. I come here to relax."

She raised her hands and stood with a smile. "You were

very subtle, but I can take a hint. It was good talking to you, Grentham. You and your people stay safe. I have a feeling the thing at Invention wasn't random and likely wasn't a one-off."

He nodded. "Could be you're right. Farewell, Ruby Achera."

She returned to find that Demetrius had won, and it was her against Liam for the next round. Her boyfriend asked, "Who was that?"

"Someone I ran across once or twice at Council meetings."

"Interesting person?"

Ruby nodded. "Before today, I probably would've said no. But yeah, I think there's more there than meets the eye."

CHAPTER EIGHT

Jared entered the secure room at Aces Security headquarters with a cup of coffee in each hand and managed to hand over his partner's without scalding himself. In a life where everything seemed to be going wrong, he counted that as a success.

Dropping into his seat with a sigh, he removed the cap from his drink to let it cool and sipped, burning his mouth. *Okay, so not a total success.* He shook his head. "You know, I never thought I'd say this, but things were better when Gabriel Sloane was alive."

His partner snorted. The dwarf, as always, was dressed all in black. His beard was a little wilder than usual, as was the rest of his hair. "I'm with you there, buddy. And I would have bet the house against those words ever sounding in this building."

"Too true. So, where do we start?"

Grentham gave a single, almost-hopeless laugh. "Invention. What the hell was that nonsense?"

"At least they didn't fire us afterward. Small blessings."

"We agree that Worldspan was behind the whole thing, right?"

Jared nodded. "Absolutely. We punched them in the mouth, and they came back with a team to get revenge. Classic schoolyard rules."

Grentham gestured, displaying his agitation. "This situation with them, we can't let it continue. The problem is, I don't see how we can take the company out. They're too big. So, unless we make the Magic City gig completely unattractive for them, they're going to keep coming back at us."

Jared frowned and crossed his arms, then let them fall when he realized he'd shifted unintentionally into defensive mode. "You're correct. As much as I hate to admit it, we can't go toe-to-toe, not right now. We'll need to hire more people, buy replacement tech, and switch up all our stuff, in case they got anything off one of our folks that would allow them to penetrate our systems."

Grentham replied, "We have initial payments from the new clients. We can use that cash to replace some of the stuff."

His partner looked concerned, and Jared knew him well enough to know he wasn't saying everything he was thinking. "Speak."

The dwarf scowled. "Bloody mind reader, you. I hate to say it, but I think we have to go to the lady Sloane and ask for support."

"Money?"

"Yeah, that. Plus, maybe to use her contacts to get some harder people than we've been hiring. If we have to face off against Worldspan, we need some ringers on our team. I have a couple, but not enough. I'm sure she knows some heavy hitters. She might even loan us some."

"You realize that would put us even deeper into her debt."

A dark laugh escaped his partner. "Man, we're so far in her pocket that we're down her pant leg to the knee."

His delivery made Jared chuckle, despite the pain of his words. "Yeah." He sighed. "How did we get here?"

Grentham gave an expressive shrug. "I have no idea where things went wrong. I'd blame the costumed jerks running around town, but aside from the thing on the Strip, they haven't directly opposed us."

"Does the change on the Council do us any good?"

"Hell no. Elnyier's the one who recruited Worldspan in the first place. That's another reason I think we may need more weight on our side."

Jared nodded and rose, almost sloshing the coffee over the edge to burn his hand, but not quite. *Still in the win column.* "I agree. I'll head upstairs and make the call."

The portal closed behind them, and Jared turned a full circle, wary of some kind of trap. There was nothing to see, though, only a bunch of pipes and pumps, all part of the oil plant Smith liked to use for their meetings. The man in question wandered out from the shelter of one of the pumps, a hand inside his coat. Jared and Grentham both lifted their hands to show they were weaponless, and Smith motioned for them to raise their arms. With a sigh, Jared complied. Grentham followed, but he could almost hear his partner mentally weighing the odds of not doing so.

Smith patted them down, then stepped back with a nod. Sloane's other lackey, Thompson, emerged from behind another piece of equipment where she'd been covering them. She tucked her gun back into its holster. They both wore dark suits, gray mock turtlenecks, and serious expressions. Smith said, "What's this about?"

Jared had only asked for a meet, not wanting to tip their hand before negotiations began. He hadn't expected Sloane to join them and hadn't wanted to seem overly arrogant by requesting a meeting directly with her. *Gotta play this one carefully if we're going to come out the other end with what we need.* He said, "We'd like to discuss the situation with Worldspan in Magic City."

Thompson's feminine laugh echoed through the place. "Oh, you mean the colossal screwup where Worldspan came in and kicked your asses at Invention?"

Grentham growled, "So you agree it was them. You seem pretty confident about it. No question in your mind?"

Smith shook his head. "None. Seems obvious what they were up to."

Jared felt anger billowing out from his partner and quickly inserted, "Well, whoever it was, whyever they did it, it doesn't change what comes next."

Thompson shifted her attention to him from where she'd been smirking at Grentham. "What's that, then?"

Jared shrugged. "Resources so we can hit them back."

Smith said, "Surely you're not asking for money."

Grentham replied, with admirable restraint, "Surely not. Rather, people, tech, and maybe some contacts."

Sloane's long-term lackey wore a weird half-smile. "Oh, is that all?"

Jared laughed, making it seem as real as he could, despite the growing sickness in his stomach. "Well, you know, we'll take whatever's on offer on top of that. Maybe you two would like to join us."

The others exchanged glances, then Thompson said, "Yeah, we figured this would probably be your angle, so we asked the boss what she thought about it beforehand." She stopped talking.

Gritting his teeth against the pettiness of making him ask, Jared replied, "And?"

Smith shrugged. "I'm sorry to say that you're on your own. You failed too many times. When you prove yourself, *if* you prove yourself, we can have this conversation again."

Grentham growled, "I very much doubt you're sorry."

Thompson put a hand over her mouth, pretending to be shocked. "You said the quiet part out loud. You're not supposed to do that." She dropped her hand and waved, taking a step back toward the exit, her other hand again on the butt of her gun. "Ta, ta, fellas. Good luck."

The last word they heard from the pair was Smith calling, "You're going to need it."

When they'd returned to Aces, Grentham had headed into his office and done some yelling, and to judge by the sound of it, broken a couple of things. In a way, Jared admired his partner's ability to express his emotions viscerally. His were seething inside, boiling in his stomach, making him nauseous. But he had no way to get them out. Yelling wasn't his thing. Casual violence wasn't either. He needed to find a distraction. *Some drinks, a beautiful woman, maybe. Something to take the edge off.*

Grentham opened the door to his office carefully as if he didn't want to slam it by accident. The dwarf said, "So, time to close up shop and get out of town?"

Jared leaned back in his chair and put his feet up on his desk, shaking his head. "No way. I like it here. You have all sorts of community connections. I've been thinking it through, and if they want to play, we'll show them how to play Ely-style."

Laughter burst out of Grentham. "Did someone replace my partner with a movie gangster?"

Jared joined the mirth. "Maybe. Just maybe. But seriously, I'm not ready to give up. We should both make sure we've prepared our exit plans, but it's not time to run. From here on out, we should consider ourselves at war with Worldspan."

Grentham snarled, "And bloody Julianna Sloane. I'll show her we can succeed at something. We can succeed at messing up her plans in Magic City."

"I'll be completely satisfied if we can get back to where we were before all this nonsense began, as long as I get to put a bullet in Smith."

His partner grinned. "A fireball will work, too. I'm happy to oblige."

Jared nodded serenely. "Either way. So long as it hurts. Smug bastard." With a sigh, he sat up straight again. "All right. Time to get to work."

CHAPTER NINE

Morrigan crouched beside Idryll on a rooftop southeast of the Strip. She and the shapeshifter were in full costume, and a magical veil concealed them from prying eyes. *And hopefully prying sensors, as well.* "I think that's the one. Agree?"

The other woman nodded. "Yes. That's the address Demetrius gave us."

The infomancer was on call, working on something for a client but aware that they were in the field. However, she didn't think they'd need his help. The data gathered from the battle against the PDA drones had provided multiple triangulated locations for control points. One was the PDA headquarters, but the other two they hadn't known about. They were out to take a look and see what the Paranoid Defense Agency was up to.

Morrigan said, "You have the locators, right?"

Idryll sighed. "You've asked me that three times now, and the answer is the same as it was the other two. Yes, I have them." The initial plan had been simply to perform recon on the sites. However, Ruby had mentioned Margrave was working on tracking devices. It had seemed logical to drop by his place and pick up the ones he'd already completed on the off chance they might turn out to be useful.

What Morrigan definitely *didn't* want to do was somehow lose them because then she'd have to listen to Ruby whine about it. *I've listened to my sister complain enough for two lifetimes.* "Yeah, yeah, whatever. Let's get over there."

They jumped across to the roof, landing carefully on the edge. Morrigan's eyepieces rotated through detection modes seeking traps and revealed a substantial power flow to a series of large boxes on the rooftop. She also spotted a camera mounted in the corner, which would've been invisible if not for the electricity it used. "Got video surveillance."

Idryll replied, "Break it? Jam it?"

Morrigan shook her head. "I've been working on something. Let me give it a try." She concentrated, staring hard at the scene before her and picturing how it would look to the camera. Then she created an illusion of that sight immediately in front of the lens and put a veil behind the image to block out any contradictory visual. "Okay, let's go around the long way and come in from the side. I think we're good."

"You think? What if you're wrong?"

"Then I guess you get to demonstrate your fantabulous skills at beating down PDA drones, troops, and whatever else they throw at us."

"I find this plan entirely acceptable." Idryll led the way over to the cases. Each was about the size of a very large suitcase, the kind you'd use for international travel, maybe even bigger than that. They were, to put it bluntly, drone-sized, perfect for the heavy combat models the PDA used.

Morrigan said, "I think we're in the right place."

Idryll pointed at another area of the building's roof, which had a small open-sided shelter with several smaller drones sitting in it. "Aw, they're cute."

Morrigan laughed. "Go tag them with the locators. I'm going to open up one of these boxes and make sure they are what we think they are."

The shapeshifter complied without arguing for a change, and the elf pulled out her knife and shoved it into the narrow seam near the top. She hammered it in with the palm of her hand, then wrenched upward, snapping the latch that held it closed. She muttered, "Not super secure. Seems like they put this on in a hurry."

Idryll had reached the smaller drones and was crouched to the side, pulling small discs out of the pouch Margrave had given them. "Probably our fault."

"We can hope." Morrigan lifted the lid and found what she'd expected to see. She closed it again, rose, and noticed the bundle of cables leading into the back of each box. She muttered, "Tag these too when you finish those," but her mind was already working. *Maybe they lead to an antenna or a communication hub? I figured all this would be wireless.*

Her surprise doubled when she discovered the cable ran down over the edge. She coated herself in invisibility and peered over the side. The line entered the building through a window on the third floor.

She almost jumped out of her skin as Idryll asked from directly beside her, "What is it?"

"Holy hell, don't do that. How did you see me?"

The shapeshifter tapped her eyepiece. "Thermal. Plus, you're on our map."

Morrigan replied, "The cable goes into a window down there. Not sure why it's hard wired, but again, maybe they were in a hurry, and that was the easiest way to do it. Or it could be a security thing. Demetrius would probably know."

Idryll said, "We should take a look."

"Yeah, I'll go down and see."

The other woman had already started climbing down the side of the building, using her claws for purchase. *Should really have anticipated that.* Morrigan covered her in a veil and waited.

After several moments, Idryll climbed back up and reported, "There's some sort of big workstation thing in the main room of the apartment, with a person behind it. I couldn't see anything else other than a kitchen and a hallway."

Morrigan scowled. "I guess that puts an end to our adventure here. Let's go check out the other building."

"It would be stupid not to take a closer look. We're here."

"Ruby wouldn't like that."

Idryll grinned. "Well, she's not here to complain, so she doesn't get a vote."

"Listen, they can't know we were here, or we lose the element of surprise."

"Really? Wow, that never occurred to me." The tiger-woman rolled her eyes to illustrate her opinion of Morrigan's comment. "Don't you have something in your bag of tricks that can help us out?" She gestured at the quiver.

Morrigan mentally ran through the options. "I suppose the knockout gas could work, but they'll hear the arrow, and when they wake up, know someone was there."

"Can you take the gas thingy off it?"

She retrieved the projectile and examined it. "It's all one piece, but you could probably use your claws to cut it off." She handed it over, and Idryll scored and snapped it. Morrigan continued, "Still risky, though. They might hear the capsule, too."

"I have a thought on that one. I've seen it on TV a ton of times. There's sure to be an air ventilation system with access up here on the roof, right?" A few minutes later, Idryll had slipped out of her costume and shifted into house cat form, carrying the knockout gas cylinder in her teeth. The plan was for her to climb down to the apartment vent and discharge it.

She'd assured Morrigan that she could hold her breath long enough to make sure it got into all the rooms. Morrigan's last comment before she'd departed had been, "If you fall asleep down there, don't expect a rescue." Idryll had only grinned and jumped down. After several minutes, her voice carried up the metal shaft. "You can come down."

Morrigan used the grapnel on her belt to slide down, then contacted Demetrius. "Hey, D, I need to get in a window. Will you check for security systems?"

His voice came back almost immediately. "Sure, hang on." After a minute's silence, he said, "Seems like there isn't one. At least, I can't find any wireless telltales. Look for low-tech stuff, magnet connections, that sort of thing."

Morrigan did all the searching she could from her position but didn't see anything. Finally, she used her force magic to unlock the window, slid it open, and stepped through. She dropped cautiously to the floor and crept around the side of the workstation to find the tech leaning back in his chair, arms hanging at his sides and mouth agape, snoring softly. Idryll joined her a couple of moments later, back in costume.

She examined the workstation setup and noticed control spots for the drones, plus several monitors and some communication gear. She keyed her comm again. "D, I have an equipment console of some kind here. Think you can do anything with it?"

"Find a place to hide a signal enhancer there, and maybe put another on the roof in case it needs additional power. Then, give me a day, and I'll own them."

"Good deal."

Idryll gave her a haughty look. "See, I told you we should take a look inside."

"Yeah, yeah, you're brilliant. Clearly, Ruby and I are holding you back."

"It's true. I really should have been chosen as *Mirra*, with Ruby as my companion."

Morrigan laughed, "It's anti-tiger, is what it is."

The shapeshifter nodded. "So true. Which is unfortunate because tigers are great."

"Remind me to introduce you to *Calvin and Hobbes* when we get back. You're going to love them."

CHAPTER TEN

Ruby walked down the street of her home kemana, seeing it with fresh eyes. Her experience attending the Council meetings had provided a new layer of understanding about the currents that flowed unseen in her community. As above, the place was full of shops, restaurants, everything the residents could need.

As far as she knew, the amount of interaction between the surface world and the kemana was unique on Earth, mainly because of the casinos. *Although heaven knows, it's not as if I'm an expert.* She felt like she should know more—as if she should know *everything* if she was going to be the leader of the Mist Elves or whatever the *Mirra* did. *But that's not important right now.*

She reached the door to Shentia's shop and pulled it open, stepping inside to find the Drow absent from her normal position. Voices came from the back of the building, both familiar and one male, suggesting the woman was with a client. Ruby adjusted the duffel bag over her shoulder, which was surprisingly heavy when carried in that particular configuration. *Give me a good back sheath any day.*

Her gaze wandered over the shelves as she wondered at the purpose of the various items, trying to think of a reason she might need them. When she spotted a necklace that was entirely too beautiful for her ever to wear, and her inner voice shouted that she *had* to have it, she gave a soft snort at her ridiculousness. O*kay, apparently, I have a weakness for magic items. Being a technomancer, that's probably not too far beyond the pale.*

Further rumination was interrupted by the arrival of Shentia and Challen, the gnome healer, from the back. Ruby hugged the smaller person and exchanged pleasantries. He offered his farewells and bustled out, carrying a backpack that looked about to burst.

The Drow explained, "At first, he handled shipments of his supplies. But eventually, he decided he'd rather spend that time enjoying himself and outsourced it to me. He gets what he needs without effort. I get free medical care for myself and a few select others. It's a good arrangement for everyone involved."

Ruby nodded. "Seems like it to me."

Shentia, who wore a long button-down black coat with a shining medallion at her neck, nodded and crossed her arms. "So, what can I do for you today?"

Ruby could feel the other woman calculating what favors she might extract in exchange for helping Ruby out. "I'm interested in acquiring an artifact sword."

That seemed to surprise her, based on her expression. "Really? I thought you had one already."

Ruby nodded. "I do, but I'm working toward proficiency in dual-wielding swords, and it seems like it would be good to have a pair." She shrugged the pack off her shoulder and laid it on the counter between them. "Here, let me show you."

Shentia had seemed about to speak but remained silent as Ruby reached into the bag with one hand and grabbed the sheath through the fabric with the other. She drew the blade, baring the steel, and held it out for the other woman to take.

With no transition at all, she was no longer in the shop. Instead, she was on the mountaintop where she'd first met Tyrsh, surrounded by stone, snow, and biting wind. The chairs she usually imagined weren't present, and she had the immediate sense she'd made a misstep. From behind her, the harsh tones of her sword's male inhabitant confirmed it. "Have we done something to offend you?"

Ruby turned to find the two entities standing shoulder to shoulder, each dressed in the most formal and reserved clothes she'd ever seen them in. He wore all grey and Shalia forest green. Both outfits covered them from the soles of their feet to their throats, and elegant button-down outer jackets that reached to their calves finished their ensembles. The pair had never looked so much alike—or so severe. She stammered, "What? No, of course not."

Shalia's expression turned questioning. "Then why replace us?"

Ruby shook her head. "There's a misunderstanding here. I don't want to replace you. I'm simply thinking of adding a second blade."

Tyrsh sounded incredulous. "You intend to wield two sentient swords at once?"

"Yes, that was my thought."

From behind her came the mocking laughter of the Atlantean who represented the artifact in her arm. "Discord in the home?"

Ruby scowled and replied without turning. "Do you really need to show up every time we three get together?"

His mirth continued unabated. "Of course I do. You have yet to allow me to train you, and you rarely, if ever, use me, so this is the only entertainment available. And it is, indeed, *highly* entertaining."

Ruby sighed and met Shalia's eyes. "I sense that I'm missing something important."

The other woman nodded. "Sometimes we fail to remember how untutored in history you are, wielder."

"I'll try not to take that as an insult."

Tyrsh laughed darkly. "Perhaps you *should* be insulted if it inspires you to learn more about the powers you attempt to control. But to eliminate the mystery, while you could possibly use two artifact swords at once, it would be a very poor choice on your part."

His companion echoed, "Very."

Ruby wasn't sure if they based their position on magic or whether these particular entities were against it. "Why?"

The Atlantean laughed louder as he moved into her peripheral vision. She turned a little to see him clearly as he replied, "Sentient magics are inherently possessive and jealous. How have you not figured that out yet, between them and me?" He held out his hands to resemble a set of scales. "To attempt to balance the needs of multiple personalities is difficult, as you've seen. To carry another artifact sword would be a heinous insult to these two. And, to be fair, probably to any inhabitant of an artifact weapon."

The others nodded as he continued, "It's not that they're especially possessive. In fact, the only thing they are exceptional at is being equal parts boring and annoying."

The pair glared at the Atlantean, and a ripple of power thrummed through the air. When it passed, only the three of them remained. Ruby said, "I didn't know you could do that. That's useful."

Shalia nodded. "Your lack of knowledge seems to be the crux of many issues. I will make an effort to educate you better and to anticipate what you need. At the current moment, you must understand that the Atlantean was largely correct. We would not welcome an additional artifact weapon. And, frankly, I don't believe there's enough room in your head to accommodate increased influence."

Ruby scowled. "Hey, leave the small brain comments to Idryll, please."

Tyrsh's laugh was lighter this time, and the mood became instantly less dark. "It is a simple statement of fact. You already find coping with us and the Atlantean challenging. Adding another into the mix would be unbearable for you, especially if it was reluctant to cooperate. Then your only solution would be to wield only a single artifact weapon, which is the situation you currently have."

Shalia nodded. "While his suggestion that we are jealous is not fully accurate, it is true that we don't wish you to replace us. You won't find anyone better for you than me." She looked at her partner and amended, "Than us."

Tyrsh added. "So, instead, perhaps consider focusing

your energies on the single blade and on learning how to maximize its use." The corners of his mouth turned down. "Even if that means working to learn what the Atlantean has offered to teach."

Ruby dipped her head in acceptance of their position. "For what it's worth, I'm sorry for the misunderstanding. I have no wish to replace you, now or ever."

They nodded in unison, and she instantly returned to the shop. Only a second or two seemed to have passed. Shentia took the weapon from her outstretched hands and said, "I have never heard of anyone successfully wielding two artifact swords. My understanding is that it's generally not done."

Ruby laughed. "Yeah. Turns out the sword is of the same opinion. They just let me know that."

The other woman smiled. "Sentient artifacts are always a challenge and a reward." She returned the weapon, and her fingertips absently rose to touch the medallion at her throat. *Perhaps she has one herself and speaks with firsthand knowledge.*

Ruby sheathed the sword again and withdrew the dagger and its sheath from the bag. She handed the weapon over and said, "I won't need this anymore. Thank you for the use of it."

The other woman nodded. "Are you sure?"

"Yes. Positive. I need to learn to cast spells through the sword and not having that one as a crutch will push me to do it. On a different subject, do you know of anything that can counter a Rhazdon artifact?"

Shentia turned solemn and shook her head. "Nothing I've ever heard of."

Ruby sighed. "Yeah, somehow I figured that would be the answer. Okay, thank you."

The Drow nodded. "As always, you're welcome. Stay safe, Ruby."

She chuckled as she slung the bag back over her shoulder. "I'll do my best."

CHAPTER ELEVEN

After spending the day in her bunker working hard on getting the small drone's payload function operational and almost but not quite succeeding, Ruby was equal parts frustrated and exhausted as she portaled into her room at her parents' house. She and Morrigan had agreed to have breakfast together with her folks the next morning, and it made sense to sleep over.

Idryll was still in the house on the surface after indicating her desire to stay there for the night. On occasion, she and the shapeshifter scraped against one another, and their snarky comments had almost risen to actual hurtful words during the afternoon's work. *My fault. Technology made me testy. I should get her some salmon to apologize.* She laughed inwardly. *No better way to influence Idryll than through her stomach.*

She'd crossed her hands on the bottom of her shirt to pull it off when she spotted the blue and silver ribbon tied through the handles of her wardrobe. Her arms flopped to her sides, and she sighed loudly. "Of course." The ribbon was the signal to come to Oriceran, and the type of knot was Keshalla's instruction to do so immediately. "Bloody hell, I'm way too tired to train."

Nonetheless, she opened the connection between the planets and stepped into the living room of her house. She walked into her dressing area and found her mentor sitting there, waiting. Ruby yawned. "I'll be ready in a minute. Just have to get my gear on."

Keshalla shook her head. "You're not here to train. Word came from the mystics. The messenger has arrived."

Adrenaline and excitement shot through her, and all traces of exhaustion evaporated. "Really? Excellent. Not knowing what's next has been eating me alive."

She was already moving toward the door when a thought struck her. "Hell, I can't go looking like this. Give me fifteen minutes." She opened a portal to her attic room in the house she shared with her roommates and poked Idryll as she crossed to her vanity. "Get up, kitty cat. Events are afoot, and you don't want to miss them."

Her companion transformed from her feline form to her annoyed humanoid one and hopped off the bed, as alert and fresh as she always seemed to be when she first woke. "What's happening?"

Ruby grabbed a couple of rings and the hair clips she preferred, then opened a portal connecting to her bedroom in the kemana. Idryll followed her through. "The messenger has arrived."

She caught Idryll's grin in the mirror on the way to her wardrobe. "Outstanding. The waiting has been irritating."

Ruby laughed as she yanked open the doors to reveal her clothes. "Right? Now, what does one wear to meet the mystical messenger?" She slid hangers to the side repeatedly, muttering, "Nope. Nope. Nope." Then she brightened, "Oh, that'll do." She pulled out a vintage dress she'd found in a pawnshop on the surface before she'd left for college. It had been loose, so even though she'd bulked up some, it should still fit.

She changed into it and admired her look in the mirror. The sleeves ended in small holes for her thumbs, ensuring that the lines stayed long and clean. It gathered in at sternum height, fell straight to accentuate the narrowness of her body, and flared out a little to accommodate her hips. It was a fabric she'd never taken the time to figure out, something between polyester and cotton but with an unexpected heaviness. The bottom was finished with lace and ended at mid-calf. It swirled when she twirled, but the weight kept it from rising at all.

She chose her best boots, which didn't have daggers hidden in them, unfortunately. She added her magic bracelets and her shield pendant, then bound her hair up high, pulling the sides straight up and back, turning the whole thing into a cascade that looked vaguely like the flourish atop a Roman legionnaire's helmet. Finally, some quick touches of makeup finished the look. She grabbed her sheathed sword and tossed it to Idryll. "Carry this, companion. Make yourself useful."

As they crossed to the other planet, Idryll complained, "Note that the title is companion, not sherpa, or servant, or even valet."

Keshalla laughed at her whining. "I think it's a reasonable ask, in this case, Idryll."

The shapeshifter grinned. "Oh, I completely agree. But my job is to make the *Mirra* better, right? So, I'm helping her improve her mental endurance."

Ruby snorted. "Well, if I have to deal with many jerks, I'll be set after putting up with you for this long."

Keshalla ordered them both to shut up and set a deliberate pace toward the mystics' compound. Ruby momentarily wondered why they didn't portal, but as members of the village fell in behind to follow them up the mountain, she understood. This was a notable event, as the last stage of the *venamisha* had been, and they wanted to be a part of it.

Nadar awaited them at the end of the path, with an unfamiliar and regal-looking Mist Elf beside him. She was tall and thin, with braided dark hair that cascaded over her shoulders and down to her waist. *The messenger, I presume.*

Ruby stopped and turned to the people who had followed her. "Thank you for being here. Thank you for always being there for me in the past." Smiles greeted her words, and she turned back and drew a deep breath. She muttered quietly, "No stress, Ruby. Just do it."

She strode forward, and Nadar tipped his head in a slight bow. "*Mirra* Ruby, welcome. This is the messenger."

The other woman also inclined her head, and Ruby matched it. She noticed Idryll and Keshalla doing the same. The messenger's voice was musical and pleasant. "Congratulations on your success."

She smiled. "Thank you. But it took all of us to make it happen, so really it's our success."

"As you say. Are you ready to assume the mantle and duties of *Mirra*?"

"Do I get to know what they are first?"

The other woman laughed. "Of course. The *Mirra* in the past have served as the moral compass of the Mist Elves."

Idryll interrupted with a muttered, "Uh-oh," and Ruby kicked her.

The messenger continued, "In addition, the *Mirra* is the final word in all disputes. When a local leader, such as the honored Keshalla, cannot resolve an issue, the people involved may seek guidance from the *Mirra*. Her word is law, her decision binding with no possibility of appeal."

The weight of that duty settled on her like a shroud. "So, no pressure."

The messenger nodded in understanding. "Those who have gone before you responded similarly. It is an awesome responsibility. Greater still is the role of the *Mirra* as the voice of the Mist Elves. You are the emissary to the other groups on Oriceran. You speak for all your people, and as with internal disputes, your word binds everyone. And now, for the first time in history, you will also be our voice on Earth."

Ruby knew in her heart that she was unworthy of such a tremendous responsibility. Her mind also recognized that every single person who'd ever stood in this place had probably felt the same. There was no way to be prepared until you had experienced it.

She believed she had a firm ethical grounding and enough wisdom to help others parse difficult issues. *And I have Idryll to rely on, and Keshalla, and the mystics, and at need, my family.* Finally, she trusted that fate or magic had chosen her for a reason and wasn't about to fight against that. "I am ready to become the next *Mirra*."

The messenger nodded solemnly. "Then, Ruby Achera, your castle awaits."

CHAPTER TWELVE

Much like the procession up to the mystics' compound, the walk up to the castle included an abundance of people. Most of the mystic community had joined the flow and were at the front of the trailing group. The castle was visible beyond the magical shield that protected it, unlike the last time she'd been there. Ruby sensed the barrier was still in place, though, and the messenger stopped before it and turned to face them. "I am sorry to say that only the *Mirra*, her companions, and the mystics may continue. Those not pledged in one of those ways are not permitted into the castle except as petitioners, and only if the *Mirra* wishes to receive them."

Ruby turned and called, "Thank you again. Whatever happens here, Keshalla will return to share the tale with you." Her mentor nodded, and the crowd seemed to accept their dismissal with good grace. She turned back to the messenger. "Lead on."

The barrier didn't fall, but they passed through it without hindrance. They walked up to the castle, which was now an off-white that still somehow shone in the sunlight. A feeling of welcome replaced the ominous ambiance present during Ruby's previous visit with Idryll and Keshalla.

Behind her, the archivist, who apparently hadn't left the compound in years, breathed, "It's beautiful."

Ruby nodded. "It truly is."

Idryll said, "Much less threatening than last time. Of course, once you're in there, no one will want to come, anyway."

She laughed, and the sound echoed from all around her. Even the messenger chuckled as she spoke. "The companions have always been the best friends and fiercest critics of the *Mirra* they served."

Ruby said, "Did you hear that, Idryll? *Served.*"

"Don't make me clunk you on the head with your sword."

Ruby asked the messenger, "It's impossible to get a new Companion?"

The other woman turned and walked backward, smiling at her. "You are not the first *Mirra* to ask that question, either. No, it is not possible. You've made your choice, and you're stuck with it."

Idryll sighed. "Dang it. I'm cursed."

They crossed the threshold into the room that had held the four statues. There was now a fifth, although it was only a figure like an artist's body positioning doll, with the small crown the others wore atop its featureless head. Ruby asked, "Why aren't the companions represented here?"

The messenger, who had stopped to allow everyone to

admire the statues, replied, "That was *Mirra* Kaeni's decision. She felt leaving them as a surprise for her potential replacement was the best choice. There is another hall where the companion statues reside, in an arrangement identical to this."

Ruby asked, "What do you think, Idryll?"

The shapeshifter answered, "Oh, definitely keep the surprise. I mean, I guess one day I'll be part of the mix, and I would much rather come as a shock to them."

She laughed. "Very well." The messenger led them on a tour of the palace. The usual stuff you'd expect to find in a place like this was all present: kitchens, bedrooms, a grand master bedroom for the *Mirra* along with an adjoining room for the companion, and several libraries filled with books and artifacts.

It also held an armory containing the historical weapons of the Mist Elves, plus several others from different cultures. A whole wing had servants' areas, with a washing room, kitchen, smaller living spaces for staff, and so on. A large empty hall ran along one side, covered by windows on both walls. Ruby enthused, "This would make an excellent training space," and Keshalla nodded in agreement.

The messenger laughed. "That is exactly how *Mirra* Kaeni used it. She would appreciate you."

"We've met, at least kind of, during the *venamisha*. I like her very much."

Finally, they returned to the main area. The messenger said, "It is time to make it official. Ruby Achera, Idryll, please stand in the center of the statues." She complied, suddenly nervous.

The other woman took a position along the line that connected the outer doors to the inner doors between the staircases, and the remaining people gathered around in a semi-circle. All except Keshalla, who perched halfway up a set of stairs with her elbows on the banister, gazing down with a grin on her face.

Ruby asked, "What?"

Her mentor shook her head. "The idea that my student, who can barely manage to fight without tripping over her own feet, is going to be the next *Mirra*? It points out the unfathomable random humor of the universe."

She burst out laughing, and the tension she'd been harboring melted away. "I suppose you're going to claim responsibility for all this." She gestured around.

"Of course. You would be nothing without me." She delivered the words with mockery that went both ways, making sure everyone understood it was a joke.

Idryll added, "Or me. Really, you'll be a figurehead. I'm the brains of the operation."

Ruby drew a deep breath and let it out, then met the messenger's eyes. "I'm ready."

The other woman nodded. "First, companion. Do you agree to serve the *Mirra* to the best of your abilities until the end of your days?"

Idryll asked, "If I say yes, does it mean I have to be nice to her?"

The messenger maintained her solemn expression, but one side of her mouth twitched upward. "No, service does not require you to do so."

"Very well, I agree."

The air vibrated at her words as if the building's magic

was cementing her commitment. Ruby recalled hearing of such oath magic in the history of the Mist Elves but had never been present for its use. *Probably just my imagination.*

The messenger turned to her. "Ruby Achera, do you accept the mantle of *Mirra*? Will you lead the Mist Elves to the best of your ability, ruling with fairness and wisdom, until the end of your days?"

This is it. Last chance to run away. Ruby nodded. "I do. I will."

The air rippled again, and the messenger grinned. "Very well." She turned to the mystics, capturing Nadar and the archivist in her gaze. "Traditionally, the mystics have acted as the staff and servants for the *Mirra*. That is, in fact, one of the purposes of their creation so long ago."

Nadar frowned. "I've heard nothing."

The archivist added, "We have no records anywhere."

The messenger inclined her head. "You do not remember because the magic of this place strips that memory when the *Mirra* is gone, and during her reign, you swear to secrecy." She smiled at the archivist. "It is, indeed, recorded, but those books stay here in the castle." She turned back to the mystics' leader. "Will you accept this charge?"

He looked back at his people, all of whom were nodding in agreement. He shrugged. "We will."

A third ripple of magic flowed through the air. The messenger clapped her hands once and turned to face Ruby. "It is done. Welcome to your home, *Mirra* Ruby Achera." She gestured up at the statue, which had formerly been featureless. Now it looked like Ruby, standing tall and proud in the dress she was wearing. The hilt of her sword stuck up over its shoulder.

Ruby said intelligently, "Wow."

Keshalla and Idryll laughed, and the messenger smiled. "Wow, indeed. Now, for your first official task as *Mirra*, you must commune with those who preceded you."

CHAPTER THIRTEEN

Ruby followed the messenger through the castle again. They entered one of the libraries, a comfortable space with several chairs, a fireplace, and stone walls covered with wooden shelves. The other woman walked to the centermost of three large bookcases wholly filled with books.

She selected a text that looked no different from the others, pulled it forward, and a latch popped. She continued to pull, and the bookcase turned out to be a door that swung wide to reveal another behind it. Ruby chuckled. "Classic."

The messenger nodded with a smile. "Indeed. The interior door only opens for one who has completed the *venamisha*, so you will have to enter first."

Ruby frowned. "What happens if I pass out, or if something bad occurs while I'm alone in there?"

The other woman's expression didn't change. "When the next person completes the full *venamisha* and unlocks it, the messenger will remove your body and give the place a thorough cleaning for them."

She scowled. "You're not particularly caring."

The messenger shrugged. "That is not in my job description."

"What do you do between *Mirra*? Wake up once a year to clean the castle and work on your horrible people skills?"

She chuckled at the insult. "I do not endure in the same way as some of the others you've seen. I was living a normal life in my village, then one day I woke up with all the knowledge I needed to handle this role and a compulsion to do so. I tried to resist for a time, but the headaches were so intense that I gave in and acquiesced."

Ruby muttered, "Sounds familiar." She sighed and said, "Okay, let's see what's behind the door." She pushed it open and discovered a small chamber, more like a walk-in closet than an actual room. In it was a single chair, facing back toward the entrance.

Her companion offered, "I believe you're supposed to sit there."

Ruby snarked, "Really? What makes you think so?" Then she turned with a sigh. "Sorry, I'm acting snotty for no reason. I might be just a *little* tense."

The other woman's expression grew in sympathy. "I sure would be if I were you. I'll wait outside until you return or until it's time to sleep. Since there is no couch in the library, I'll occupy the nearest bedroom on the left as you exit into the hallway. Please come find me at need."

Ruby asked, "Will I be able to get out of here?"

She shrugged. "One imagines so."

Ruby turned to the chair with a sigh as the door closed behind her. She didn't fail to note that the messenger had never actually stepped across the threshold into the room. *Smarter than I am, probably. Of course, if you believe Idryll, that group includes almost everyone.*

The chair itself was oversized, carved from dark wood. It was more like a throne, with a heavy base supporting the seat, back, and armrests. Cushions covered the appropriate areas. She sat, finding it strangely comfortable, and waited. Nothing happened. After almost a minute, she said, "Okay, what's the deal? Let's get this show on the road, people."

The woman she'd seen depicted in the first statue appeared before her. She wore the same outfit as the marble version. While it had looked somewhat archaic there, on this apparition, it seemed soft and supple. *Maybe a fabric representation of leathers, to honor tradition while setting herself apart from the normal look of those she ruled?* "Hi. I'm Ruby Achera."

The woman dipped her head in a nod. "Hello, Ruby, I'm Inshala. I imagine you're at least a little confused."

She laughed. "More than a little."

The other woman's smile was almost matronly, even though she didn't seem much older than Ruby. "It was the same way with all those who preceded you, and most so for me since I was the first."

"If you were the first, how were you chosen?"

"Excellent question. My companion, Ransha, was sent to find me. Whatever magic made all this possible decided we should be together."

"He's the rock guy."

She nodded. "Indeed. We descended into the mountain and faced challenges similar to those you experienced, but not quite the same. When I was named *Mirra*, I altered them in a variety of ways."

"So, what is all this?"

Inshala replied, "I deemed it important that there be some continuity from one *Mirra* to the next. However, since I had no way to be sure I could physically speak to whoever came after me, I created some magics to assist. Now, each new *Mirra* has the opportunity to talk to those who've gone before." She smiled. "I believe that's enough for me. We can talk another time if you wish."

She vanished, and an instant later was replaced by a man. He was not much older than Ruby was, to judge by his smooth face, where the only wrinkles were laugh lines around his eyes. Ruby introduced herself, and he said, "I am Cashri. I was second *Mirra* of the Mist Elves."

She asked, "What was that like? No pressure, am I right?"

He laughed, and the earnest sound suggested he had done so quite a lot when he was alive. "Indeed so. Although my time was more than a century after Inshala, so there were no particular expectations. In fact, when the summons for the initial *venamisha* came over me, I was thought to be diseased.

"My village took me to the mountain, as they did with all our people who were near death. This was so that when we passed on, we would be forever in its embrace. But once I was alone, my headache disappeared, and I felt the pull. I'm sure you know what I mean."

Ruby nodded. "I do. I didn't expect or understand it when it hit me, either."

"I chose my companion, and we ventured on through

the trials, eventually succeeding. I was visited by Inshala, although neither this chamber nor the castle existed at that time. She agreed it was unfortunate that knowledge had not passed down from her time, and so I made it the goal of my life to ensure some level of continuity for the *Mirra*.

"While handling my other duties as leader, I created the order of the mystics and put them to work building both their compound and this building. Neither was complete before my time was over, but when I left the mortal realm, I was confident they eventually would be."

Ruby admitted, "I always thought the mystics were a bunch of crackpots who didn't want to be part of the normal order."

He laughed. "Well, people can be more than one thing, right? The monastic life lends itself to certain personalities. Almost always driven, often rebellious, and usually seeking some knowledge they can't quite put their finger on. I put funds in place to support their needs and chose the first leader with great care, making sure to select someone of like mind who would continue what I had begun. That, essentially, is the end of my tale. Farewell, until we meet again."

He vanished, and the other male she'd seen in the statues quickly replaced him. His face was round, as was his body, and he introduced himself before she could. "Hello, welcome to the club. I'm Mintel."

Ruby laughed. "Thanks. Ruby Achera. So, you were the third *Mirra*?"

He nodded. "Indeed I was, and, I guess, am. I benefited from Cashri's efforts, so when the *venamisha* called me, I recognized it for what it was. Many had gone before me, of course, but none had completed the trials. I didn't know that then, but once I succeeded, I gained that knowledge."

Ruby frowned as she tried to understand the big picture. "So, people are always trying? But the success rate is so low that a *Mirra* appears only once in a long while?"

Mintel shrugged. "I can't claim to understand the will of the magic. But I don't believe that's the case. I think, instead, that pivotal moments in our history trigger the calls. Basically, when we need a ruler, the magic seeks to find one."

Ruby sighed. "That doesn't bode well for the current moment."

"The same was true in my time. After a long period of prosperity, the Mist Elves were fragmenting. Villages were disconnecting from one another, becoming more tribal and standoffish, and even talked of leaving the mountain and expanding through Oriceran. The *venamisha* had given me a strong conviction that we were where we belonged and that moving to other parts of Oriceran would be a bad choice."

"That sounds like an extraordinarily difficult situation. How did you deal with it?" Ruby had no idea what she would have done if that was her challenge.

"I redirected them. Earth had become close enough that it was possible to reach it, and I had some skill in portals and magical navigation. So, I led those with the desire to wander to the other planet and charged them with learning it for our people. They were happy, and the requirements set by the magic, or those who had gone before, or both, were served. I was the first to be able to inhabit the castle, and I decided to create this chamber within the library as a hidden place the *Mirra* could retreat to."

"It's kind of small. Not really the greatest hangout."

He nodded. "Very true. I wanted it to be secret, so I had to build these walls myself. I am not the best mason."

Ruby laughed. "*Mirra* of all trades, huh?"

"Indeed so. When my time ended, I believed I had delivered us from the great danger and counted myself a success. Hopefully, history still considers me one, as you no doubt will be. Farewell, until we meet again."

He vanished, and finally, a familiar face appeared. Kaeni smiled at her. "Congratulations on your success."

Ruby said, "You remember me?"

She nodded. "In this altered life, we can make new memories. I know you from the trial."

"Were you also summoned at a pivotal moment in our history?"

"The magic called me as Rhazdon emerged. It was before they rose to prominence, so I was unaware of the purpose until much later. I instituted our policy of complete non-engagement with the rest of Oriceran and increased our connection to Earth, knowing that our people might one day have to flee there."

Ruby nodded. "That makes sense, from everything I know about them. But what am I supposed to do?" She felt she could be honest with the other woman as if they had a relationship. *My new bestie is a ghost. Awesome.*

Kaeni shrugged. "Lead. Find out what needs doing, and do it. If you have been chosen at a pivotal moment, to use your words, you'll need to figure out what it is. The good news is that you start with the same wisdom any of us did because times change so much between *Mirra*. It's always new. And remember, you can come and talk to us whenever you desire counsel."

Ruby asked, "Are you alive?"

Kaeni shook her head. "Think of us as a deep pool of memory that can act somewhat like the living beings we were. We are far less than you but far more than recorded memories."

"How did you get that way? Will I be that way?"

Kaeni laughed. "For the second question, yes, you will. It is part of being *Mirra*. For the first, kneel facing the chair."

Ruby complied, and Kaeni said, "Now put your thumbs in the two notches shaped like crescent moons and press to the sides."

She pushed, and a drawer opened with a click. She pulled it out and found the circlet she'd seen all the *Mirra* statues wearing. "What is this?"

"The means to store your memories."

Ruby removed it and stood, pushing the drawer closed again with her foot. "Does it hurt?"

"Not at all. When you put it on, you won't even notice it's there."

Ruby drew a deep breath and set it on her head with no small amount of trepidation. Magic swirled through and around her. She reached up to verify the circlet was still seated properly, but it had vanished, apparently merging with her. She frowned. "This is a poor time for jokes."

Kaeni laughed. "If not now, when? In any case, that is the last step. You are officially the new *Mirra* of the Mist

Elves. Until you need me again, I bid you farewell, and the greatest of luck, Ruby Achera."

She faded before Ruby could thank her, so she headed for the door. "This thing better open because if it doesn't, I'm gonna haunt everyone. There won't be enough Ghostbusters on either planet to deal with the harassment I'm going to hand out."

CHAPTER FOURTEEN

Jared finished packing up the heavy roller crate and attached the top, snapping the closures with annoyed twists. "I hate this." They were in the garage, making sure they moved out all the important and expensive equipment. They'd already relocated half of the vehicles, and Grentham's gang would be removing the rest in short order.

The dwarf said, "Yeah, I hear you. Hopefully, it's all for nothing."

Jared scowled and gave the crate a hard push, sending it rolling across the floor toward another of Grentham's people. The elf maintained a portal that connected to one of the dwarf's warehouses, which would be their temporary base of operations until the thing with Worldspan was over. "Oh, there's no way they can resist striking back at us. After we walked in and messed with their facility? You know they're looking to return *that* favor. And without Sloane's protection, they'll certainly feel emboldened to do so."

Grentham paused what he was doing and looked up. "You don't think it's just that the boss lady isn't in our corner, right?"

Jared shook his head. "No, we're totally on the same page on that question. She's now in the opposition column along with Angelina Prash and the rest of Worldspan." He grabbed the next of the big rolling crates and moved it into position. "You know, our numbers are looking pretty low for this."

Grentham nodded. "Any other time, not having a bunch of people hanging around headquarters would be good. Means they're all out on gigs, which is where we want them. But if Worldspan decides to attack, we will definitely wish they were here. Still, gotta keep the cash flowing, right?"

Jared nodded. "Now more than ever. There's bound to be some added expenses from all this nonsense."

"Well, if they do decide to hit us, they're in for a surprise. A bunch of them." A number of his people emerged from the portal and Grentham directed them to take over the loading. "Let's you and I go make sure the other things are the way they should be."

Jared tossed what he was holding inside the crate and walked along with his partner. Their first stop was the armory, which they'd stripped of all its weapons, and all the lockers emptied. He shook his head. "Now that is a sad sight."

Grentham turned to the pair of dwarves sitting on the benches. "So, is our plan set?"

Jared recognized the first from their attack on the Worldspan headquarters. Veara said, "We're good. One of the two of us will be awake and located here at all times. We'll be on comms even when we aren't on the clock. When things go down, we'll open the portal, and our people can rush in from the warehouse."

Jared nodded. They'd decided it was a nonzero possibility that Worldspan would just blow up the place without entering, so having a welcoming party inside was a bad idea. Everyone hoped that their drones, which were monitored off-site, would be able to detect a substantial attack on the building's exterior early enough that the dwarves could escape.

Grentham clapped the other dwarf on the shoulder. "Good work. Stay frosty."

Jared touched his comm. "Claire, where are you?"

She replied, "Main hallway, just past the conference room."

"We'll be there in a flash." Jared followed his partner toward the front of the building. They'd decided that only a couple of rooms would remain in use to perpetuate the illusion that things were normal at Aces. They'd still welcome clients in the lobby, and they'd still talk to them in the conference room. Once past that area, the rest of the place would be heavily trapped. They found his most trusted lieutenant and Grentham's most capable trap person, Karna, working on that defense. Jared asked, "What's the plan?"

The dwarf replied, "Well, fortunately, we have really good sensing in here already. It's smart that you all didn't scrimp when you put in that stuff. Now it's time to connect the demolitions to the sensors. We're using a mix of tools.

Incendiaries, gas, claymores, and even some old-school crossbow traps."

Jared asked, "Won't they have shields?"

Karna laughed. "That's the best part. Some of these traps also use anti-magic emitters that we, uh, borrowed from the PDA."

Grentham chuckled along with his subordinate. "Resourcefulness is one of our specialties."

Jared shook his head with a smile. "I don't want to know. Anyway, sounds good. As long as the anti-magic is localized so it doesn't interfere with the other parts of the operation that require magic."

Karna replied, "We have it under control. We dialed them way down, just far enough to catch the people in the kill zone."

Grentham grinned. "Such a good phrase, *kill zone*. Pretty much this whole place is going to be one big KZ by the time you finish. Keep it up."

Jared said, "One more thing. Secure room." He grabbed the box full of jewels and tucked it under his arm. "Can't forget these."

His partner sighed. "Opening ourselves up to tracking, if they're magically tagged."

He nodded. "I'll take them to the bank and put them in a secure deposit box. It's not great since I don't have deniability if anyone gets a warrant, but I doubt the people who will be looking for them are the same kind who are likely to have a judge sign off on their actions."

Grentham nodded. "Sounds good. I think everything's as prepped as it can be, but I'd feel more comfortable with a little more overwatch."

Jared nodded. "I was thinking the same thing. Scimitar?"

"Yeah. Let's give her a call, see if she can hack into Worldspan for us. It would be a hell of a bonus to know right when they were coming."

They returned to the garage, careful not to interfere with any of the traps being built or the ones already in place, and found a quiet corner. Jared instructed the comm to connect to the infomancer, and a moment later, her computer modulated voice replied, "Yes?"

"Jared Trenton, as you doubtless know. We'd like to contract you for a gig."

Even through the electronic distortion, the woman's tone held a note of regret. "I'm afraid I cannot accept. In fact, I will be returning your retainer for this month and the one before. Since we were not actively engaged in a project, I accepted another. Unfortunately, it's exclusive, so I can't take work from other clients."

Jared's stomach sank into his feet, and Grentham replied with a muted snarl, "Any clients? Or just this one?"

The infomancer didn't respond, and Jared asked, "Is this about money?"

She answered with a tinny laugh, "Isn't everything?"

"That's not an answer."

The computer modulated sigh was a strange sound. "Let's simply say that there are only a few people I see as potential threats to my health and welfare. Unfortunately, it is one of them who has requested my services. It would not be prudent for me to decline."

Grentham asked, "And the exclusivity comes from them?"

"Affirmative. I'm sorry, gents. Once this is all over, I would welcome the opportunity to work with you again."

The line dropped, and Jared sighed. "We're going to need a new infomancer. Hell, to make up for her, we might need two or three. And I have no idea where we're going to find even one anywhere near as good as she is. Heaven help us if she's working for Worldspan."

A thought occurred to him. "Dammit, we need to change everything. She has our accesses by now, even the ones we didn't share with her."

Grentham nodded. "You're right. I'll get my best person on it, but we're going to have to hire more." Where Jared felt abandoned by someone he'd kind of trusted, his partner's response held nothing but anger. "We're being boxed in. Next, they'll probably start peeling off our clients and suppliers. I've seen this nonsense before, and it only gets uglier."

He grabbed a wrench from a nearby table and threw it across the room. "Assuming we survive whatever happens in the near term, things will have to change. Long term, if we still want to be around, we need to find some new allies and take the fight to Worldspan, Sloane, and anyone else stupid enough to come at us."

CHAPTER FIFTEEN

Paul Andrews and his number two, Charlotte Krenn, were seated in a back corner table, as far from the entrance as possible while still distant from the kitchen doors. He always preferred to choose a defensible position and carried a pistol in his shoulder holster and a Taser at his hip, just in case. A drone watched over the restaurant's entrances, and a human was monitoring the feed. *Can't be too careful, but can't let myself be trapped in the office, afraid to go out, either.*

The eatery was a barbecue place a couple of blocks south of the Strip, frequented by humans and magicals alike. Mostly, no one cared that he was there, although a few dark looks were thrown his way, presumably because of his species rather than his position. *I shouldn't be that recognizable yet. If I was, that would be a problem.*

His dining partner set her water glass down on the table a little harder than normal, and he realized his thoughts had distracted him. He said, "Sorry. Just thinking about how hungry I am."

She laughed. "Maybe you need to get a little more work-life balance going."

He grunted. It was a common joke between them, as neither of them had much of a life outside work. The gig in Ely was different from their usual postings because they didn't live within walking distance of headquarters. In the other cities where they'd been together, including Reno, they'd taken apartments in the same building or one nearby to minimize time lost during the commute. "So, bring me up to date."

She nodded and leaned forward so no one overheard them. He'd paid extra to ensure the tables to either side would remain empty, giving them some privacy. *Or the illusion of it, anyway. One never knows what magic might be happening around them.* "We have three committed to going after the bounties. Actually, that's a bit of a misleading statement since they're a team."

He adopted a quizzical expression. "Really?"

She nodded. "Yeah, I hadn't heard of them before either, but I went and looked them up. They call themselves Dante's Angels, and while some folks online have posited that they're sisters, I'm not buying it. The few pictures I found showed one was blonde, one brunette, and the last a redhead, and their facial structures aren't particularly similar. I think they're going for the *Charlie's Angels* reference."

He laughed. "Was the intermediary named Bosley?"

She shook her head with a grin. "The world really is stranger than fiction, isn't it? Anyway, rumor has it that they're good. They've done several legit bounties, mostly low-level but a couple of mid-range. Plus, between you, me, and the wall, some suspect they've taken on a few less than lawful gigs as well."

He sighed. "You know, before we came to Ely, that probably would've bothered me. At this point, it feels like a bonus. So, only three who are one?"

She nodded. "The costumes are only level one bounties. Not too much demand for those, as the pay isn't great. We did put out the word that there was extra cash involved on top of the bounty, which is what brought in the Angels."

He kept his tone neutral. "Only level one, you say?"

Her voice took on an edge of defensiveness. "We couldn't invent major crimes, you know?"

"Why not?"

His matter-of-fact answer set her back, and she was silent for a moment. Finally, she explained, "Too easy to trace, too likely to generate suspicion. It would be bad if someone found out we were messing with the bounty system. We want to stay under the radar."

He grunted, knowing she was right. "We still need to get more of them."

Charlotte replied, "I know. I'm on it. It'll take a little longer than we'd hoped."

"In the meantime, make sure we have tabs on the Angels at all times. Plant tracers on them if they won't do it voluntarily, or task a drone."

"You're using them as hunting hounds."

He spread his hands and looked from one to the other as he spoke. "Best case, they handle it themselves. Worst case, they lead us to the costumes, and we make the move. Either way, we win."

She gave a single sharp nod. "I'll keep teams on standby, then, and make sure the drone ops are ready."

He leaned back and stretched his arms over his head. "In the meantime, I think I'll see if the Council will put me on the agenda for their next meeting. Might be useful to stir the pot a bit on that front, too."

The following night, Ruby crouched on a rooftop to the extreme south of the city, her companion beside her. Demetrius said in her ear, "Normal activity all around. Seems like the PDA is in wait and see mode."

She chuckled. "I hear that tone in your voice. Don't you dare start poking at them."

He laughed. "Why not? It's fun."

Ruby shook her head with a grin but didn't reply. The infomancer had used the access Morrigan and Idryll had provided to penetrate the agency's drone network. He was pretty sure that, at need, he could mess with the signal flow and cause the pilots to lose control at a minimum and possibly even take over the crafts.

They were keeping that option in their back pocket because if they didn't do it perfectly, the PDA would know they'd been hit and would respond by upgrading their systems. At this point, information was what they needed.

She stiffened as a group of people came around the corner Demetrius' drones had pinpointed as a location the Drow and his gang often passed through. As Morrigan had put it, "It's been too quiet for too long. Something's bound to happen," which was why they were staking it out. Her sister was at Spirits, ready to deploy and likely annoyed at her assignment.

When Ruby had explained that one of them needed to stay back in case the other two got into trouble, she might not have been completely sensitive to the fact of her sister's prior kidnapping. It was the sort of thing she might've intentionally done when they were kids, but this time it was a screwup. *Well, she'll get over it. Seems like talking with Challen has been helping her deal with the stress.*

Idryll said, "Hey, the scumbag in the hat is here." Ruby's attention returned to the group below, and sure enough, the Drow in the fedora was in the middle of the procession. At least a dozen people walked around him, and while they weren't moving quickly, they nonetheless had a sense of purpose about them.

Ruby observed, "This looks like more than an evening stroll. Tree, get some visual coverage going. Mo, you might want to move to your departure point."

Her sister replied, "On it."

Her boyfriend reported, "I sent the drones up. Our super-secret feed from the PDA still shows no activity in your area."

Idryll said, "It would be nice to be able to beat down this bunch without an audience."

Ruby laughed. "Please. You *always* want an audience." She kept them covered in a veil as they paralleled the Drow's team. As they neared the Strip, she started to wonder what the hell was going on. "Correct me if I'm wrong, but does it seem like they're trying to attract attention?"

Demetrius replied, "If that was their goal, they've

accomplished it. PDA drones have altered their patterns, and additional ones are spooling up."

Idryll ventured, "Maybe we won't need to intervene."

Ruby responded, "Double-digit magicals versus drones? The robots don't stand a chance. It's kind of turning out to be an expensive month for the PDA."

Morrigan laughed. "Serves them right. Their drones are making everyone nervous. Want me to join you? Looks like you'll be going past my location."

Ruby frowned, part in confusion and part in annoyance over being confused. "No. Stay back. This is too weird. We might need you to get us out of jail when it's over."

Idryll added, more darkly than usual, "Or the hospital."

She killed her comm. "You feel it too, then?"

Her companion did the same. "Yeah. They're looking for trouble and seem serious about finding it."

"That's my read, too." She flipped her comm back on. "Tree, give Alejo a heads up through the usual channel. She'll be able to get emergency services primed for whatever is about to happen."

Morrigan asked, "Are we going to try to stop them?"

"As much as I'd like to, a preemptive strike plays into the bastard's hands. He'll claim we're working for the humans, and since we've coordinated with Alejo in the past, he might be able to make that stick. No, they have to act first. But we won't waste a second after they do."

A few moments later, the group took a turn that made it apparent where they were heading. Morrigan exclaimed, "Holy hell. Taka Tower."

The sense of danger she'd been feeling doubled. Taka Tower was Ely's tallest non-casino building, topping out at twenty stories. The condos within provided a gorgeous view of the Strip and the mountains, and it was home to the wealthiest humans in the area. It was an eminently logical selection on the Drow's part. "Tree, set off the fire alarms, call for an evacuation, do whatever the hell you have to do, but get that place cleared out. Bomb threat, if you have to."

"On it."

Ruby made a difficult choice. "Screw it. We're going in, regardless of how the bloody Drow wants to spin it. Morrigan, get your butt moving."

Her sister replied, "Save some for me."

Idryll snarked, "Not if I can help it," and leapt from the roof, landing cleanly three stories below. She charged at the rear of the troublemakers' formation, which had spread out to form a semi-circle facing the tower.

Ruby shook her head, urged, "Move fast, Mo," and followed her impulsive partner into battle.

CHAPTER SIXTEEN

Ruby took stock of the situation as she ran toward Taka Tower. The attackers—since their plans were clear at this point, she felt comfortable naming them as such—had formed double ranks. Those facing the building were already almost in range, and the ones walking backward to guard against those who might intervene were aware of their presence, judging by their actions. Fireballs flew at both her and Idryll, forcing them to break off their direct rush and circle.

She reinforced the magical shield surrounding her body, then mentally reminded herself about the capsules underneath her costume on her shoulders—health on the left-hand side, energy on the right. That had seemed the most logical placement to avoid accidentally triggering them. Idryll had a pair as well, attached to her fur under her equipment belt. *It'll be interesting to see how that turns out.*

She threw a force blast at the ones who'd attacked her, but their shields intercepted and dispersed it, and more attackers joined. "Well, being outnumbered makes everything so much more fun."

Idryll replied, "Take out the back rank, or blow through them?"

"We have to protect the building. These idiots are obstacles. Knock them out if you can on the way past but focus on the others."

"Got it."

Ruby's instinct was to take to the air, but the calm, rational part of her mind pointed out she'd be awfully vulnerable while soaring over a bunch of enemies. *Damn it, Idryll, if you'd waited a little longer, we could've approached under a veil.* Still, they would've wound up in the same situation, maybe with a couple of the bad guys down, so it wasn't a huge game-changer that her partner's enthusiasm sent her running into the fray. *Like always.*

She layered force shields around herself and ran, no longer worried about actively defending against the ones in the back. She trusted her magical defenses to absorb whatever they threw while she burst through to the front line. She lost sight of Idryll as she careened into the attacker on the end, slamming bodily into him and sending him flying toward the building.

Ahead, residents flooded out of the emergency exit doors on the bottom level. *Good work, Tree. I owe you another date for that.*

The shapeshifter asked, "Nonfatal?"

She ground her teeth together in frustration, really wanting to be able to give a different answer. "Yeah. We have to try to stay clearly on the good guys' side of things."

Morrigan, her tone dark and serious, remarked, "Even if it kills us?"

Ruby replied, "Right up to that line, but if you have to do it to survive, do it. Now, shut up and fight."

Idryll performed a series of acrobatic moves to avoid blasts of fire and shadow from the back rank of enemies as she closed. She ran directly at one and vaulted over him, using his presence to dissuade his partners from attacking her. A somersault in midair allowed her to land and run without sacrificing speed, and she wound up only a few feet away from a front-row attacker, a dwarf who held growing balls of flame in each hand.

"I don't think so," she muttered and planted her lead foot. She channeled all her momentum into a torso twist that brought her knee up at his ribs, made vulnerable by his dramatically upraised arms.

She quashed the instinct to smash him in the head. Ruby was right. Killing meant losing the support of Alejo, which they couldn't do if any other option existed. Her knee smashed into his ribs and shattered them, sending him to the dirt, keening in agony.

She threw herself to the ground and rolled as the dwarf next to him reacted quickly, taking the fireballs she'd been generating and whipping them at Idryll instead. She managed to avoid one entirely, but the other gave her a burn that extended from shoulder to knee on her left side. Fortunately, her magic deflector had consumed most of the blast, and the resulting wounds weren't bad, just painful in that unique way that burns could be.

She popped up and rushed the dwarf, but her advance turned into a frantic evasion as a shadow sword appeared in her path. Her instincts threw her to the ground again narrowly in time to avoid the slash of the second blade, and she rolled up with her claws extended. The Drow had lost his fedora, but it was unmistakably the one they'd met in the warehouse.

Purple swords smoked in his hands, magic coming off them as if they could barely contain his power. The edges looked as sharp as any blade she'd faced. He said calmly, "Go away. I have no conflict with you. Our objectives are more aligned than opposed."

Idryll growled, "Attacking noncombatants is unacceptable. Always. Period."

He glanced over his shoulder and gave a half-smile. "Seems like most of them are out of the building. Wonder how that happened?"

She touched a claw to her forehead in a mocking salute. "Guilty as charged."

The Drow reset his feet, shifting to a combat stance. "Last chance. Leave. It's only property damage at this point. No reason for you to die here today."

Idryll shook her head. "Can't guarantee that everybody's out. You and your minions could depart peacefully, though."

He twirled the swords once. "Seems as if we're at an impasse."

"Seems like."

He didn't offer any more words, simply charged in and

swung his blades at her face and torso. She danced nimbly back and let them pass a few inches away from her body, then tried to slip in and slice his arms.

A sword disappeared, and a blast of force smashed into her, his speed and power both unexpected and impressive. She flew backward as though she'd taken a punch from a giant, her chest combining surface agony with an instant deep ache, but managed to land on her feet and slide to a stop.

Idryll slammed her fist against the healing capsule under her belt and shuddered as it banished the pain of her burns and went to work on the fire in her chest. "Okay, buddy, if that's how you want to play it, let's see how many pieces I can slice you into without killing you."

Ruby spun toward the next in line, a Drow male who she momentarily misidentified as the leader. *No, that would have been too easy.* She ignored the shadow bolts he dispatched at her, trusting her defenses to absorb them. The magic deflector consumed the first salvo, and her shields dealt effectively with the second.

She grabbed one of Margrave's flash-bang grenades from her belt and threw it, looking away as it detonated. Two lightning grenades followed as fast as she could dispatch them, and when the blast finished, the enemy was down to five in the back row and two in the front, plus one engaged with Idryll.

The pair attacking the building stayed on task despite her efforts and threw two fireballs each. They slammed into its walls and set the exterior ornaments, flags, and a large banner proclaiming Taka Tower had been voted the best housing in the city, alight. Stone flew out as the impacts damaged the walls. The attackers immediately started gathering up magic for their next volley.

Ruby was in mid-rush toward them when her legs flew out from under her. She fell to land on her hands, her feet in the air. *New fitness craze, mid-combat push-ups.*

She twisted to find that the one she'd initially sent flying had snagged her with a shadow rope, wrapping it around her shields somehow, and yanked on it hard enough to bring her down. Force magic severed the line, and she smashed him with another blast of it, knocking him down again.

She popped to her feet and spun back in time to see the second round of fireballs smash into the building, blasting out more sections of the walls and intensifying the flames that had already taken hold. Ruby gathered up her magic and threw ice at the conflagration, but she'd never been strong with that element. *Plus, it's two on one, and they have a head start.*

She switched tactics and launched a dart at the nearer one's face, hoping it wouldn't turn into a "lucky" shot and hit him in the eye. Fortunately, it struck him in the cheek, and he wobbled and fell. Then she dropped to her knees as simultaneous attacks from several in the rear ranks washed over her shields.

This is going perfectly. Not. At least we've reduced the number of enemies. Demetrius shattered that belief, announcing, "Drones incoming, ten seconds, want me to delay them?"

Ruby growled, "No. We can handle this. Morrigan, where are you?"

The answer was an arrow plunking into the middle of the trio who had attacked her, its sonic discharge dropping them to the ground. Her sister arrived at her side and helped her up, and Ruby slapped the energy potion capsule, letting out a satisfied growl as the power flowed through her. "Okay, let's finish these guys."

Unfortunately, Demetrius's estimate had been uncharacteristically incorrect. Drones swooped in and attacked and forced her and Morrigan into evasive moves. Suddenly, unexpectedly, Ruby pitched backward and fell as triple blows slammed into her chest. Her breath exploded out of her, and she sat on the ground stunned and trying to inhale as three women in matching tactical gear came into focus, rifles in their hands.

She coughed and forced out the hoarse words. "New enemies. Anti-magic bullets. Watch out."

CHAPTER SEVENTEEN

Morrigan moved to help her sister, but Ruby waved her off. She spun instead toward the identically clad trio, drawing a knockout gas arrow and nocking it before her turn was complete, then launched the projectile at them. Bullets *thudded* near her and forced her to run for cover, but the arrow hit exactly where she'd intended.

In an uncanny mirror image, each of the three calmly reached into a pocket on their vest, withdrew a small mask, and fitted it over their mouth and nose. A thin black tube led back into the protective gear. Morrigan muttered, "Dammit," and drew a lightning arrow. She pulled the string back and was about to release it when her brain processed the fact that she had drawn the wrong one, selecting the heavy-duty version that would probably kill her targets.

Returning it to her quiver would be wasted time, so she twisted and shot the nearest PDA drone out of the sky. Particles rained down on the magicals in the front row, distracting them momentarily after their third volley. The tower showed signs of wear, and if they didn't get the situation under control soon, they would have a full-fledged fire on their hands.

She grabbed the three lightning discs from her belt and hurled them in sequence, one for each enemy. A wave of the center one's hand sent the objects flying back at Morrigan, which forced her to drop the arrow she'd selected to redirect them with her force magic. "And they're magicals to boot. Probably hiding pointy ears under that amazing hair."

Each had what she thought of as supermodel's hair, long, well taken care of, and full of body. Their coifs dramatically moved as they lifted the rifles as if they'd brought their own perfectly positioned breeze. Frankly, it made her jealous. *I'm not embarrassed to admit it. I have hair envy. So what?*

She drew the sonic arrow and sent it their way, but it met a wall of force that halted its flight no more than halfway there. Then she was forced to run again as their rifles chattered. "You know, these folks would fit right in with Diana and company. Except for the part where they're playing for the wrong team."

Ruby groaned. "That's not a good sign."

Morrigan jumped over the low wall that surrounded Taka Tower's inner courtyard and paused to catch her breath. "No, no it's not."

Idryll heard her partners' conversation, but the words didn't stick. She was hard-pressed to fend off the Drow, and he had captured her entire attention. Her opponent was a spinning dervish with the swords, letting them vanish at times to cast other spells, then seamlessly bringing them back into existence an instant later.

His magical pool, or whatever gives him power, must be deep. Or he's on an energy potion high. She'd heard of drugs that could increase arcane prowess as well but wasn't sure if those were real or just late-night commercial nonsense.

In any case, his assault kept her busy, dodging, ducking, and occasionally managing to sneak in a hit or a slice. One of his arms bled enough that he'd have to do something about it before too long, and she considered that a great success given the situation. But it was clear that unless she could intercept his swords and not lose a hand in the process, she wasn't going to beat him.

Idryll shouted, "Jewel, switch."

Ruby replied, "Affirmative," sounding a little hoarse, and Idryll poured on the speed, running as fast as she could in an arc that would take her past him outside his likely strike range. He turned to follow and met Ruby's sword coming down with both of his, smoothly accepting the change in partner. Idryll spotted the ones that Morrigan must've been talking about, on the far side, and had a moment of indecision, weighing attacking the magicals pouring fire into the building against going after the odd trio of newcomers.

Demetrius solved the problem for her by announcing, "PDA drones seem to have retasked to target the Drow's group. Disengage if you can."

Morrigan's response summed the situation up well. "That's a little easier said than done, my friend."

Idryll charged at the similarly clad women, and the one nearest her dropped her rifle and fast-drew pistols from each thigh. Without slowing, Idryll partially transformed to increase her speed, her body growing faster and stronger in a matter of steps, and she leapt for the woman. The guns barked, and bullets raked along her sides, but she'd narrowed the distance quickly enough and unexpectedly enough that she was inside her foe's defenses. The other woman had long, straight, blonde hair and a stylish mask covering her eyes.

Her nose was pretty, and Idryll chose it as a target, snapping her head forward to smash into it while her hands controlled her opponent's arms so she couldn't bring the guns in. The blonde fell back with a curse, her voice strangely melodious despite the vitriol spewing forth. The next closest, a brunette, slammed an elbow into Idryll's head, knocking her stumbling to the side. *Ow. Wench hits hard.* She transformed the stumble into a cartwheel, then dove behind a decorative bench as bullets from the woman's rifle sought her.

Morrigan growled, "Find new cover," and Idryll scrambled away as the bench ripped off its moorings and flew at the women. It deflected up and over them and forced the archer to smash it to the side before it reached where she stood behind a low wall.

Idryll said, "Okay, there's some competence there."

Morrigan replied, "Right? These people suck."

Ruby snarled, "Keep them busy but work toward the edges. I'm going to see if I can portal this guy back to the bunker. The moment I say go, Morrigan, you get Idryll out of here."

Ruby momentarily wished that she had two swords as her opponent used his pair to keep her at bay. The healing capsule had taken away all the damage from the bullets, along with most of the pain, but she felt the natural fatigue that came with using the potion. Her single advantage was that his hands were both occupied, and her empty one gave her options. She was out of lightning grenades and didn't want to try an explosive, so her belt had nothing to offer. But the dart gun that she'd moved to her left arm after returning the dagger to Shentia had possibilities.

She coated that hand with a thick layer of force and grabbed one of his blades as it came by. Her magic fought against his as he twisted the blade to break her hold. She strained her muscles, pushing for the right angle, then depressed the stud to fire the dart. The projectile whipped out, and he jerked his head to the side just in time for it to miss.

He observed conversationally, "Well, that was unfair." His voice was as condescending, smooth, and confident as she remembered.

She disengaged her sword and slashed it low, and when he jumped over it, tried to cut upward. But his blade was already coming down in a crescent block to bat it away. She growled, "What the hell are you doing, attacking a building full of innocent humans? You *can't* be that stupid. Any positive opinion you've built up will turn against you because of this."

He let one of his swords vanish and cast ice at her. She crafted a shield of fire to absorb it and stabbed through the conflagration, hoping he wouldn't be able to see the attack coming, but his sword intercepted it, nonetheless. *Damn, he is good. No wonder Idryll wanted to switch. We might have to go two on one to beat him.* Unfortunately, she could see that her partners also had things going on.

Ruby muttered, "Okay, here we go." She released magic into her muscles as she dodged, parried, and deflected, readying herself for a final attack. She reached for her power to create the portal, and suddenly it all fell out of her grasp. SUVs screeched into place, and PDA troops barreled out wearing their damned backpacks. Ruby shouted, "Disengage, go, now." She spun away from her opponent and ran.

Demetrius's words came fast. "They have some really good jamming going on. Jewel, duck." She complied immediately, throwing herself to the ground in a shoulder roll. A PDA drone hurtled over her head to smash into the nearest SUV, bursting into a small bonfire and causing the agents to drop into cover. He said, "Northwest, two blocks, there's a car waiting for you."

She pelted in that direction, sheathing her sword and running all-out. A chopper flew in as well, probably the same one they'd seen before, with some sort of orb mounted on the bottom. She panted, "Is that what I think it is?"

Demetrius answered, "You should be out of range of the backpacks, so if you can't do magic, I'm guessing it is."

Morrigan growled, "Damn, where do they keep getting these toys?"

Idryll reached her with Morrigan still half a block behind. They turned the corner and confronted a bright yellow minivan. She ran for the driver's side door, unable to contain a chuckle, even in the dire situation. "Really? This is the best you could come up with?"

Demetrius replied, "It was the nearest thing I could hack. Beggars, choosers, you know the drill."

Idryll slid the side door open and Morrigan dove inside, then she swung up into the passenger seat.

As Ruby got the vehicle rolling, she told Demetrius, "Thanks, sweetheart. I definitely owe you a date."

Morrigan dropped to her back on the bench seat behind her and panted. Finally, she said, "Hell, I think I owe you one too."

Idryll chuckled. "Ruby's probably not willing to share."

Her sister coughed and let out a soft groan. "I need to run more. Anyway, how about it, D? Ready to upgrade?"

Ruby shook her head and drove, hoping the PDA had been busy enough with the Drow and his people that they wouldn't pursue the rather conspicuous escape vehicle. "We have any trailers, Tree?"

"None that I can see. I think you're clear. But as soon as your magic returns, pile out and portal. I'll send the car back where it belongs."

Ruby nodded. The anger inside her was growing with each passing second. "I don't know who those three were, but it seems clear that Andrews was waiting for us to go after the Drow, using him as bait."

She shook her head, considering the implications of the new strategy. "I was happy to coexist, but apparently Andrews doesn't see that as an option. We're going to need to take the fight to him."

CHAPTER EIGHTEEN

Julianna Sloane stood on her balcony, gazing down over the Vegas Strip and out at the sunset over the mountains. Melancholy suffused her as she contemplated how much Gabriel would've enjoyed the sight and what a life they could've had together if his obsession hadn't resulted in his death.

Hindsight made her wish she'd spoken more strongly against his plan. Still, he'd always needed her to be his unquestioned support, the one person he could trust to have his back, regardless. So, in the few moments where she might have cautioned him, she'd remained silent.

Now I'm alone. Those bastards are going to pay for taking him from me. Every single one of them owes me blood. I've been letting the pot boil slowly for a while, so they'll think they've got an understanding of the things that threaten them. But it's almost time to turn up the heat to full.

Her watch buzzed with a message from Thompson, saying she was on her way up. Julianna sighed, finished the whiskey in her tumbler, and headed back through the transparent sliding door into the coolness of her apartment. When her lieutenant entered the room, she was seated on the couch with a fresh glass. She gestured for her employee to take a seat diagonally from her. "So, Vicki, what do you know?"

The other woman smiled. "Many things. Some of which you'll find *very* interesting."

Julianna straightened a little at that. "Oh, really? How lovely. Let's start with the boring stuff, though. What's going on with Aces?"

"Smith has the place under surveillance around-the-clock. We have a few drones up, and he's watching from a hotel room on a tablet. I take over now and again so he can sleep. Being tired makes him cranky." Julianna laughed at the joke, and Thompson continued, "From the outside, nothing seems to have changed, although they're not meeting as many clients at the facility as usual."

"After the debacle at Invention, that might be a lack of business. That couldn't have helped their reputation."

Thompson's head bobbed. "Could be. But they have magicals on the payroll, so they don't really need to use the doors to meet with people. It's my bet they're fully aware of the danger and are taking measures to deal with it."

Julianna asked, "Do you think they understood the message that their failures have become unsustainable where we're concerned?"

Her lieutenant laughed. "I'm sure of it, especially since they reached out to Scimitar and she turned them down."

A satisfied smile crept across her features. "Foolish of them to rely on a contact we provided in the first place. Of course, they had no way to know that Gabriel funded the infomancer's career until she was ready to break out big on her own. That sort of thing breeds loyalty, even among business partners."

She shook her head, remembering her husband talking about what a good investment supporting Scimitar would be. It was a serious money loser for a year or two, but equipping the woman and helping her get up and running had indeed been worth it in the end. The infomancer had been able to scale up marvelously quickly because of it and had served them well on any number of occasions since. "Any word on Worldspan's plans?"

Thompson shook her head. "We made some inquiries, gentle ones as you requested, and Prash was completely unwilling to share. Apparently, she prefers to keep things secret at the moment."

Julianna swirled the ice in her glass and watched the ripples. "In character. She's a proud woman."

"Or maybe a paranoid one. In any case, she did admit they're going to move sooner rather than later."

"We'll let her reluctance to reveal her plans stand for now. If they succeed in destroying or taking over Aces, it will be worth having trusted her. If they fail, we can always take a more active stance in the future. Do you see any need for us to be involved in that operation?"

Thompson shrugged. "We might gain a little intel if we pretended to be on Aces' side again, assuming they were stupid enough to trust us, but frankly I don't think Worldspan needs any assistance. Unless Trenton and Grentham come up with something impressive, it's unlikely they'll be able to go toe to toe with the other company. Worldspan is bigger, and by reputation, meaner. There's a reason they're considered the best, I guess."

Julianna nodded. "Acceptable. Just in case, start looking around the companies in town for someone to replace Aces if things with Worldspan don't work out. Ms. Prash might perceive she has more power than she does when this episode is over, and we will need options in hand if she becomes difficult."

Thompson patted her jacket over the spot where her ever-present pistol rested in a shoulder holster. "We *always* have options."

She laughed with genuine pleasure. "I love your confidence and the fact that you've never once failed to back it up with action. So. Tell me the news."

"There was a fracas last night. An attack on the Taka Tower."

Julianna was silent for a moment, surprised. Then she said, "Gabriel and I had planned to live there. The penthouse, of course. Someone was already occupying it, but we figured we could entice them to move or remove them against their will."

Thompson shifted her weight, seeming uncomfortable, but her tone was still light. "Well, after what the band of anti-human magicals in town did to it, you might want to wait a few months for the soot to clear."

"Is it destroyed?"

"No, but the fire was pretty big before they got it under control, and I'm sure that smoke seeped through the whole place. Plus, they'll have to make some serious repairs in places."

Makes sense. Unfortunate. It was a beautiful building. "Was anyone killed?"

"No. The fire alarms went off before the attack started. Lucky break."

She snorted. "No such thing, I'm guessing. Did our vigilantes turn up?"

Thompson chuckled. "They sure did. As did the PDA, with drones and in person."

Julianna was amused. "That must've been a mess."

"No video is available, unfortunately. Even Scimitar couldn't retrieve any. But we did get a still image I think you'll find interesting."

The other woman held out her phone. Julianna took it, then chuckled at the picture. "The Dante girls. Really. That *is* amusing."

Thompson accepted the device back with a nod. "So, you're aware of them?"

"Gabriel and I made it a point to know all the bounty hunters who might be coming after us. It was always easier to buy them off rather than deal with their investigations and pursuit. We mostly ignored those three, though, because they weren't in our league. Although," she said thoughtfully, remembering, "We did contract them for a non-bounty thing through an intermediary once if I recall properly. Were they after the vigilantes?"

"Turns out, all three costumes are now level one bounties."

Julianna laughed. "Really? That's an impressive play. Potentially a stupid one, but impressive nonetheless. Who's in charge of the Paranormal Defense Agency there?"

Thompson had the answer at hand. "Andrews. Paul Andrews."

"I remember hearing his name in Reno. Is he behind it?"

"Scimitar says it was the PDA, yeah. She also said that Ely PD is essentially the cybersecurity version of Swiss cheese and that, quote, a sloth typing with two fingers could break into their systems in ten minutes."

Julianna snorted in amusement. "Well, that doesn't speak well of the Ely police."

Thompson agreed, "It does not. Anyway, the vigilantes escaped, and the Angels faded. The police made some arrests but missed the leader."

"So, failures all around? Well done indeed." She thought about the situation for a full minute, appreciating her subordinate's recognition of the need not to interrupt her.

Finally, she said, "You know, I think there's an opportunity here. Contact those three and inform them I'd like to layer another contract on top of the one they're on. Working for Andrews will give them a certain amount of access that we wouldn't have otherwise, and I intend to use it."

Thompson nodded. "Will do. And if they ask what we need done?"

Julianna grinned. "Once they accept, you can tell them they'll be taking on the Council. It's time to move into the eye-for-an-eye phase of the operation against those who took my husband from me."

CHAPTER NINETEEN

Ruby stilled her features as she followed her father toward his seat in the Council chamber. She'd immediately spotted Paul Andrews standing in the opposite corner, deep in conversation with the new Council leader. She took her place behind Rayar, then leaned down and asked, "Is that who I think it is?"

He glanced over and nodded. "Elnyier warned us he'd be here. Andrews, director of the local branch of the Paranormal Defense Agency."

Ruby shook her head and replied automatically, "Paranoid Defense Agency, more like. Strange to see him down here. I thought I was the only human allowed in the kemana."

Her father chuckled at her joke. "On occasion, we invite others. You know how it is." He shrugged. "Besides, it would've been very inconvenient for all of us to go up there. He better mind his manners, though, or someone might accidentally portal him to the World In Between, rather than back to the surface."

Ruby shuddered. The mention of that hellish dimension never failed to scare her. "Even if he's as bad as everyone says, that would be too evil."

If her father had intended to respond, the opportunity vanished as the last members flowed in and took their seats. Elnyier nodded to the assemblage and said, "Thank you all for coming. I know it's strange not to have Maldren here, and I appreciate the support of those who have reached out since I was elected. I promise I will do my very best to respect and represent the enormously diverse viewpoints around this table."

Ruby's eyes were on Grentham as the woman spoke, and she noticed his lips slightly moving after she finished speaking. *Wonder what he's saying to himself. For as much as he thinks she's a better choice than Maldren, he doesn't look at all happy.*

The Council leader continued, "Our guest is the head of the local office of the Paranormal Defense Agency. He requested a chance to talk to us, and given all that's been going on in Magic City, it made sense to acquiesce. Director Andrews, the floor is yours."

He took a few steps forward from the corner he'd been leaning against. "First of all, thanks for the opportunity to speak to you. I know it's rare for someone from the surface to be a part of your deliberations. I very much recognize that allowing me to attend was a decision not lightly made. Respecting that, I won't waste your time.

"To put it bluntly, we need to stop the magicals who are stirring up anti-human sentiment. My preference is that the Council would step up, do its job, and police your own. If you choose not to, however, I will handle it for you.

Either way, though, it gets handled. I wanted to make sure that was abundantly clear."

Murmurs and side conversations sounded in response to his words, and Elnyier slapped a flat palm down on the table. "Council people, please. Let's maintain some decorum here, shall we?" She locked her eyes on the Kilomea. "Bartrak, it seemed like you had something to say. Please share."

His bass rumble replied, "Very well. It is rather bold of this man to attempt to dictate terms to us when he is busy persecuting our people on the surface."

Andrews crossed his arms. "Care to explain that accusation?"

Bartrak growled, "Drones everywhere. Your troops responding with, shall we say, *enthusiasm* to the idea of 'policing magicals,' as you put it."

The agent shrugged. "That's our mandate, and have no doubt. We will live up to it as circumstances require. What I'm suggesting is that you alleviate our need to do so."

Andrielle said, "So what you want is for us to do your job with no compensation?"

Andrews let one hand fall to his side and gestured at the assembly with the other. "Seems to me that as the major landowners in the city above, you have a vested interest in keeping things calm. Do you really think it'll be that long before your human-hating troublemakers spill over onto the Strip and mess with the tourists you need to make your places profitable? I mean, the recent escalation should have been a clarion call to you all."

Elnyier replied neutrally, "You're referring to Taka Tower?"

He didn't quite snarl, but it was close. "Of course I am. Attempting to burn down the building with people still inside? That's a dangerous step in the wrong direction—way over any acceptable line. So, I guess you should consider this your fair warning that I won't tolerate such things any longer. If you're not going to take care of it, I will."

Ruby's father, Rayar, replied, "Isn't that why we have a police department? And a sheriff's department?"

Andrews shook his head. "No, you have those organizations to handle the problems they're qualified to handle. When it comes to magical mischief-makers, you get to deal with my people and me. We, at least, understand how outclassed we are from the get-go and are properly equipped to level the playing field in a way local law enforcement can't."

Grentham replied, "That's a very authoritarian stance. Don't you think you might be overstepping?"

He snorted. "Those sound like the words of the Drow in charge. Oh, wait, sorry, the Drow in charge of the *street gang*. Guess I should be more specific."

Elnyier's tone and inflection remained unchanged. "That comment was beneath you, Director Andrews. I believe you have made your case. Please leave by the main exit, and one of my staff will see you safely home." He nodded, suddenly looking concerned as if he realized he might've misstepped. Nonetheless, he departed. She said, "So, that was interesting."

A couple of chuckles greeted her words, but even they were tinged with anger. Bartrak, in particular, seemed to be barely restraining fury. "My people are already tired of the presence of the PDA in the city. We want them gone. Perhaps, if his focus is on the anti-human movement, eliminating it would be the best path to that end."

Elnyier shrugged. "Agreement, disagreement? Other opinions?"

The conversation continued for twenty minutes, resulting in no action other than everyone recommitting to keeping their eyes open and sharing information. Ruby's attention stayed locked on Elnyier throughout the proceedings. The woman seemed almost sleepily calm, completely removed from the issue at hand. *That's strange. The first big challenge of her administration, as it were, and she's treating it like it's nothing. I wonder why.*

After returning home, Ruby changed clothes and joined her father and mother in the study for a drink. Rayar opted for whiskey, but she and Sinnia chose hot chocolate, complete with a perfectly toasted marshmallow in the center. She ventured, "So we know what Andrews thinks about the Drow and his anti-human movement, and the Council seems unwilling to act, more or less. What's the gossip in the casinos?"

Her father said, "All sorts of talk, none of it good. I know this sounds crazy, but if you ask me, I think someone has taken up the reins Gabriel Sloane dropped when he died."

Her mother nodded. "I agree. This thing with the Drow whipping up a frenzy is just too coincidental. Feels like it has to all be part of the same big picture."

Ruby sipped her drink thoughtfully. "I'm not sure I agree with you. I don't see how violence in the streets benefits whoever's playing the role of the Nightmare. They're probably connected, but cause-effect doesn't quite ring true for me."

Her father shrugged. "We have too little information."

"What can I do to help?"

Rayar said, "As Ruby Achera? Maybe hang out at the casino more often and see if your ears pick up things ours don't while you're working the floor."

A shiver ran through her at his tone. That was the first part of a two-part statement, and she feared he was about to reveal she'd blown her cover as the city's defender. Instead, he continued, "As *Mirra* of the Mist Elves, it might be time for you to start throwing your weight around."

Relief washed through her. "Where? How?"

Her mother laughed. "Seems to me that's up to you, oh great leader. I'm sure you'll figure it out."

Ruby rolled her eyes. "You should be more respectful to me in my new, auspicious position."

Sinnia stuck out her tongue. "To me, you will always be the little kid who used my lipstick as battle paint on her face and pretended she was a Kilomea." Her mother's eyes sparkled. "I'm not sure Dralen has ever recovered from being hunted through the house against his will."

Ruby laughed. "Yeah, I had my moments of rottenness as a kid, it's true."

Her father raised an eyebrow. "As a kid?"

She scowled at him. "Okay, enough wandering down memory lane. The leader of the Mist Elves has important, nay, vital things to do." She stood and stretched.

Her mother asked, "Oh really? What?"

A yawn delayed her answer momentarily. "Get some sleep. Honestly, Council meetings are so boring I almost passed out in the middle." She waved as she left the room, her parents' laughter following her down the hall.

CHAPTER TWENTY

After breakfast the next morning, Ruby spent the morning with her family, something she hadn't been doing much lately. She planned to spend the afternoon and early evening with her roommates, who she'd also been neglecting. Late evening would be time for patrol with Idryll.

Her plans upended when she received an afternoon text from Prex, the head of the Desert Ghosts motorcycle club.

Probie twenty-three, your presence is required at an event this evening, beginning at nine p.m. We will be at the compound all night, so plan for it.

She'd known something like this would be coming along, like she knew that eventually, Shentia would ask her to perform additional tasks to work off the debt she owed. Prex had explained when she joined that the club could call upon her when it wanted her, and her choice at that point would either be to acquiesce or resign. She'd come to appreciate the group members and saw herself staying aligned with them for as long as she was in Magic City, so the second option was right out.

Ruby sighed. "Guess patrol is off the table. Idryll is going to whine."

She dressed simply in jeans, boots, a white T-shirt, and a leather jacket. Her sword she left behind, but she took her pendant and shield bracelets. Plus, she was now always wearing two of Daphne's capsules. They were almost unnoticeable, and it would be foolish not to.

By the time she arrived, the celebration was already well underway. Prex had a wide grin on his face and exchanged a double fist bump with her. Ruby asked, "What's the deal?"

"We're having a party. First shift of servers has finished. Now it's time for the probies to go to work."

"Seriously?"

He nodded, and his voice had a challenging edge to it. "Beneath you?"

She laughed. "No, not that. I'm just clumsy as hell and rarely meet a bottle I don't manage to break."

He laughed and punched her in the arm. "You'll fit right in. Get to it. People are thirsty."

Ruby found the other probies, a female gnome, and a male elf, and they divided the area among themselves. She made sure she had Prex's group under her auspices so she could continue the banter they'd begun. The gig was simple. She walked around, asked people what they needed, and delivered it, whatever it was.

She wound up running bottles of beer, going into the

compound's kitchen and carving up fruit for mixed drinks, ordering over a dozen pizzas during the evening, and collecting empties and pitching them into recycling bins.

It took her about twenty minutes to get into the flow, and for the rest of the night she circulated, laughed, and worked hard. Not once did any of the larger issues in her life cross her mind. The evening was, in a word, blissful.

People started falling asleep at around three in the morning, and by the time the sun rose, only a few of them were still awake. She sat beside Prex and said, "Anything I can get for you, boss?"

He laughed. "You know, you claimed you weren't good at this, but it appears you were fantastic at it. Everyone seemed to enjoy themselves."

"You have a great group here. Work hard, play hard. That's the way it ought to be."

A smile stretched his face, and he gestured around him. "I'm lucky to be a part of this. I'm reminded of that in some small way every day. But you know what it's like to care about your community."

She nodded. They usually didn't discuss her costumed activities, but she'd never told him not to or anything. Since no one else was in earshot, she had zero concern. "Seems as if it's all fracturing a bit at the moment, though."

He grunted. "Grentham informed us of the change in Council leadership. I didn't love Maldren, and I don't love Elnyier."

"You'd prefer to see him in the role?"

Prex shrugged. "Chances are he'd be okay at some of it, but he doesn't really have the personality for the gig. He'd say the wrong thing to the wrong person at the wrong moment, and we'd find ourselves in some kind of a giant mess."

"Seems like there are a bunch of hotheads on the Council. Elnyier, though, as near as I can tell, is made of ice."

He replied, "I don't know her except by reputation, but that tracks with what I've heard."

"What else do you hear about her or whatever?"

"A lot of people are asking questions on the street about the Council members and their families."

"Really?"

Prex scratched his beard. "Yeah. Consensus is that some of those making the inquiries are PDA, which I guess makes sense. They have to suspect the anti-human thing has an inside connection."

She frowned since that thought hadn't occurred to her. Not at a conscious level, anyway. "Really? Why is that?"

"The heat gets turned up by one Drow, and suddenly another Drow is in charge of the Council? It's not a particularly sophisticated calculus, you know?"

Ruby chuckled at his phrasing. "Okay. If that's your evidence, I'm sorry to say it fails to live up to any actual empirical standard."

"Whatever. I'm not saying they're in it together because they're Drow. I'm just saying I think she's an opportunist and would be a fool to ignore that situation. People under stress always cling to a leader who seems strong, right?"

"I believe I've heard that sentiment once or twice from people who should know."

He tipped his beer bottle toward her in acknowledgment. "The more concerning part is that my folks say that it's not all PDA. That magicals are asking, and even some masked folks." He stared at her hard, any pretense of intoxication vanishing.

She lifted her hand. "Not me, not my companions, promise. I couldn't care less what the Council does, as long as they don't screw things up more than they already are."

He said, "Really? Ruby Achera, fake human and new leader of the Mist Elves, doesn't care about the Council?"

She blinked and thought about denying it, but the confidence with which he delivered the words let her know there was no point. "How'd you find out?"

He laughed. "Well, first, I'm not stupid. The Mist Elf face you're wearing now has some vague similarities to the human Ruby. And you were never all that good at responding to the fake name you gave us when you wanted us to stop calling you Dragon Lady. Slipped once or twice when you heard something that sounded like your real one. I might have even done it a few times as a test."

"Yeah, I kind of suck as a liar."

He rolled his eyes. "Says the person who pretended to be a human for most of her life. What's up with that, anyway?"

She sighed. "It's all very dramatic. My parents believed a prophecy of a sort could have referenced me. That made them worry about my safety, so they came up with this elaborate ruse. Might've been easier just to pretend I was a boy or something."

"I'm not sure how much of you is an illusion and how much is real, but I don't think it would be easy to mistake you for a boy."

A laugh burst out of her. "Are you hitting on me?"

He grinned. "Not my type. You're too tall. But you have exquisite," he looked her up and down, "bone structure."

She shook her head but couldn't stop smiling. She'd noticed before that he treated sex like it was something funny, and frankly, that attitude worked just fine for her as long as it didn't offend anyone involved in the conversation. "Bone structure, huh? That's what you're going with?"

"Yep."

"Okay, then. I'll have to ask my boyfriend if he likes my *bone structure*."

Prex nodded authoritatively. "Hundred bucks says he does."

Ruby shook her head. "Anyway, now you know. Is it a problem?"

He shrugged. "That's the thing about being part of the Desert Ghosts. We don't care about your baggage, and we don't care what you do when you're not with us as long as you're not a scumbag. So far, probie, you fit in just fine. But I guess I have to ask. Now that you're all fancy and stuff, are you planning to leave us?"

Ruby laughed. "Hell no. I love you people."

"Good. Because we've got another party scheduled next weekend, and you've made yourself invaluable as a server."

"Doesn't my noble status earn me anything?"

He nodded solemnly. "It does get you one thing."

She replied, "What?"

He grinned. "Well, since you come from a rich family who owns a bloody casino, you're springing for drinks at the next one."

"Counteroffer: I spring for drinks, but I get to attend. I'll serve at the one after."

"Deal, but you have to buy pizzas, too."

Ruby chuckled. "Spoken like a natural negotiator. Done." They closed the deal with a fist bump and leaned back in their chairs to watch the sunrise together.

CHAPTER TWENTY-ONE

Angelina Prash knelt in the middle of her office with her weight settled back on her heels. In her mind, she systematically eliminated all the distractions of the day, setting commonplace worries aside. The night to come would be decisive.

It wasn't her first battle, far from it. However, it was the first time she'd invaded the headquarters of a rival business. Part of her felt discomfort at the idea. She noted the emotion and let it fly free. The die was already cast, and what followed was inevitable.

She opened her eyes, then stood. Her team was deploying from their new temporary headquarters in Magic City, an industrial plant on the edge of town that had fallen into disrepair. They'd already transported all the necessary gear. All that was left was for her to join them, don her battle armor, and give the word.

Her partner wasn't taking part in the evening's adventure. His responsibility was the business side of the company, making deals and watching the books. The action end of things was her domain. *Time to hold up my part of the bargain.* She grabbed the leather jacket that went with her tight leather pants and opened the portal to Ely.

After the incident at their headquarters, Angelina wasn't taking any chances. She had more people than she needed, six teams of four plus herself and a guard to stay at her side. Each team had at least two upper-level employees who oversaw operations on the ground for their clients.

The plan was to hit fast and barrel through the place to knock out any opposition before their target could react. She was completely aware the other company had to know they were coming. *Unless they're idiots, and I don't think that's fair to assume.* That reality didn't worry her. Worldspan hired the best, and when they knew traps might be present, her experts generally found them. *When they don't, we pay a benefit to the next of kin and hire a new expert. Hopefully a better one.*

Angelina had always maintained a certain emotional distance from others. Biographies she'd read suggested that powerful people, along with highly accomplished ones such as artists and scientists, often felt the same. Like they didn't quite fit in, as if there was a gap of understanding between them and the rest of the world.

Once upon a time, that had bothered her. She'd come to terms with it, though, and considered the ruthlessness it inspired to be an advantage in her line of work. It was also one of the reasons for the division of labor she shared with her partner. *Each of us plays to our strengths, as it should be.*

The arming room was chaos compared to the serenity of her office. Magicals of most varieties talked, joked, and cursed as they donned their gear for the operation. She crossed to the tall rolling cabinet that held her equipment. It opened to her palm print, and she dressed quickly, already a minute or so behind the others.

She zipped her jacket up to the throat and put her vest on over it. The ballistic protection was custom fitted for her and extended farther down than the ordinary version. Her belt went on next, and she slid her pistols into thigh holsters after checking to ensure she had anti-magic rounds loaded. Healing flasks slotted into straps behind the guns, just in case.

Angelina strapped on protective armor at elbows and knees, plus longer plates at upper arms and forearms, with a similar arrangement on her legs. The result was something between a Special Forces unit and a football team's equipment. A bandolier with grenade canisters attached went over it all, and a rifle on a strap connected to her vest at the optimum height for her to grab it.

The new version of their eyewear, an upgrade over the ones Aces had stolen, finished the ensemble. She tapped the high-tech watch on her left wrist, triggering the self-diagnostic system of her comm and instructing it to interface with the glasses. A moment later, she had a stream of data on one side of her visual field, including minute-by-minute status updates from their drone watching the Aces facility.

She drew her pistol, pointed it at a dartboard on the wall, and put the slightest pressure on the trigger. A dot appeared where the bullet should hit, which reassured her that her sights were as they should be. The accuracy improvement provided by the infrared targeting would give her people one more edge they probably wouldn't need.

Angelina locked the cabinet again, then turned to the woman who would be her escort. "We ready?"

The Kilomea nodded with a wide grin. "Yeah. Ready to stomp some fools."

Confidence suffused her, and she laughed with pleasure. "You said it, my friend. Round these people up and let's get to it."

The assault strategy had been war-gamed several times, refined after each, and finally, they had it as well planned as it was likely to get. The Aces facility had a securely fenced area in the rear, and while that would arguably provide a more concealed means of entry, she didn't think anything would fool the Aces people at this point. From their first step into Worldspan's Ely headquarters with malicious intent, they'd set a course with this moment as the inevitable result. So, she and her team had decided going in the front would be the best choice.

Angelina had suggested blowing up the building without entering, but her partner had disagreed. She wasn't sure if it was because he wanted vengeance of a more personal kind or if his avowed reasoning, to steal back their gear and take whatever Aces had, was the driving force. Despite his calm outward persona, he could be viciously ruthless when necessary.

Ultimately, it didn't matter. By the time they finished, Aces would be nothing more than dust. They opened a portal to the front of the building and organized into their attack formation.

She nodded at the glass door, which was in the center of a whole wall of windows. *Probably all bulletproof, not that that's going to do them any good.* "Team one, do your thing." The magicals in that group ran forward and made a semi-circle around the entrance.

A member was tasked with unit defense and called up a shield in front of them with small gaps his teammates could fire through. A second sent a wave of ice at the doors and windows that fronted the Aces lobby. A moment later, the third and fourth team members dispatched blasts of force, each taking half of the frontage. The net result was a blizzard of frozen glass shards flying into the lobby and nothing standing in the way of their entrance into the facility.

Angelina ordered, "Teams two and three, take half and check for traps." She didn't need to give the orders. Everyone had memorized the opening moves. They'd planned the operation down to the smallest detail, and she'd briefed her people and tested their recall.

Reinforcement never hurts, and it gives me something to do when what I really want is to fly in there at full speed and find that bloody dwarf. Just because she felt disconnected from others didn't mean she was dispassionate. She'd happily spend an hour slicing into Grentham's flesh, applying copious amounts of lemon juice, and listening to him beg.

They quickly cleared the obvious traps, pressure plates connected to a pair of retractable turrets in the ceiling. Her team located the backups as well, intersecting beams of infrared that would also set off the defenses. After a minute and a half, they were clear to proceed.

As they'd planned, three teams went left, and three accompanied her to the right. The blueprint that Julianna Sloane provided had allowed them to analyze the most likely trap locations meticulously. It was amazingly detailed and showed heavy remodeling of the interior of the building. *Her infomancer must be sharp. It would be seriously difficult to get this amount of data on our place, and I don't think the Aces people are stupid about cybersecurity.*

She found herself smiling in anticipation and shifted back into her neutral game face. "Okay, people, remember, stay focused. Our primary concern at this point is locating traps without setting them off. Once we meet opposition, we take down said opposition and continue. No restraint required."

She stayed behind the first two teams and ahead of the third. As much as she'd prefer to lead from the front, she knew her value. Getting caught by a trap because she was overeager would be an incredibly stupid epitaph for a radically successful career.

Finally, they met opposition. A group of four magicals set up an angled crossfire out of two offices, popping alternately out of the doorways to fire, then ducking back before a counterattack could catch them. They played their hand too early, allowing her people to evade the attack.

Angelina scowled. "Amateur hour. Time for them to learn drywall isn't any kind of protection." That was all the cue her teams needed.

Three of the four front team members fired force blasts at the walls concealing the Aces defenders. The fourth protected them, holding a pair of Kevlar plates hovering in mid-air to interpose against any decently targeted gunfire. In only a moment, the walls were down to splintered studs, and their enemies were fully visible. Team two cut them down in a hail of bullets.

She shook her head. *Idiots.* "Good job, people. Keep moving."

As they progressed, she had to admit she was impressed with the defenses the Aces people had organized. If not for Worldspan's superior technology and the skills of her magical trap finders, some of the moves her opposition had made would've been downright devastating. As it was, she lost an entire team on the other side of the building to some sort of homebrew explosive trap involving an oxygen cylinder. Several members of team three on her side wound up perforated with long nails after a trap that had remained dormant and unnoticed armed itself after they passed.

Everyone had healing potions, so the injured nearest her would be back in action before too long, but the loss of the other group angered her. She'd logically known that it was unlikely they'd all come out the other end safely. That rarely happened in an operation like this. But she'd still hoped for that outcome, apparently, and was offended at having her hopes dashed. She snapped, "Do we have them yet?"

The infomancer who was riding along on the operation replied, "No. They disabled the security system."

"You can't re-enable it? There's no way their people are as good as you." It wasn't a false compliment. He was exceedingly effective at what he did, and to have him admit being unable to accomplish something was almost unprecedented.

"When I say they disabled it, I mean they physically unplugged the cameras and sensors that used to be part of the system. My guess is they have a different setup running, one they installed just for this purpose."

She nodded. "So, what you're saying is they knew we were coming."

"Of course, just as you expected."

"Think it's a trap?"

The infomancer sounded doubtful, another unprecedented moment. "I couldn't say."

A familiar voice came through speakers set in the walls as Grentham replied with a growl, "Oh, it's most definitely a trap, Angelina."

CHAPTER TWENTY-TWO

Jared shook his head with a small smile. "You can't help yourself, can you?"

He and his partner were in the garage, a spot his partner had selected as their fallback location. They'd been near the front of the building earlier, and he'd been the one to trigger the oxygen canister explosion that had taken out a number of the invaders. Jared had insisted on being part of the defense, and Grentham had agreed on the condition that they stayed together. *Suits me fine. A little magical protection is always a nice thing.*

The traps they'd installed hadn't worked nearly as well as hoped. None of the magical or sensor-triggered versions had been effective. Only the ones his people physically set off had remained undetected, and they were hodgepodge, improvised efforts at best. They'd managed to slow the invaders but failed to reduce their numbers significantly.

Grentham replied, "What? She's a wench, and she needs to know it."

Jared sighed but didn't answer. They'd retreated to the

garage several minutes before, and their infomancer provided continuous updates about the invaders' progress. Their people had punched holes in the walls and run cables to cheap cameras hidden throughout the facility since the possibility of Scimitar gaining access to their regular system was too high. They didn't know she was working for the other side, but they couldn't afford the risk. Grentham said, "Better take your position and give the order."

Jared nodded. He tapped his comm and said, "Vacation time, people. I repeat, vacation time." It was the signal for the defenders to find a safe spot to portal out of the building.

He moved to the opposite end of the garage, where they'd prepared a bastion for him on the room's left-hand side. They anticipated the enemy would use the main door in the center of the inner wall. He had a heavy SUV for cover, as well as some stacked crates and toolboxes.

Grentham and any members of his team that hadn't left yet would stand on the right side and draw the invaders' attention. As long as they didn't let the Worldspan people get behind them, they could easily skirt around the back and portal out, protected by the vehicle. It was a good plan, but they'd assumed there would be more defenders with them.

The Aces troops had fought bravely, but the Worldspan people outmatched them from the start. Grentham had ordered them to retreat when wounded rather than continuing to fight, and most of them had made it out of the building or to their last-ditch positions before he gave the order to evacuate. They both assumed the enemy leader would want some personal payback with Grentham. In fact, their plans depended on it.

When the door opened and someone who wasn't Prash appeared, Jared was momentarily alarmed. Then the leather-clad warrior stepped through with a disappointed look on her face. She said, "Really? Just two of you?"

Grentham laughed. "I only see two of you."

She grinned, showing teeth. "Give it a minute. My teams are cleaning your people's blood off their boots."

Jared shook his head. "You're mighty cavalier over a bunch of unnecessary deaths."

Her voice held a scowl that her face didn't reflect. "I didn't see you shed any tears when you blew up my building with people inside it."

"We knew you'd escape. And most of your people were already out when the 'gas leak' went up."

"My initial inclination was only to wound yours, but I'm afraid my folks got a little excitable. Seems they dislike you rather intensely."

Grentham said, "That's okay. They'll get what's coming to them, eventually."

Prash shrugged. "This conversation is boring and stupid, just like you. Finish this, Dreana." The Kilomea ran toward Grentham, who sent a fireball at her.

Prash interposed a force shield to protect her partner and pulled up her rifle one-handed. She waved it in Jared's direction with the trigger depressed, and he ducked to avoid the barrage. He rose again in time to hear the blast of Grentham's shotgun and enjoyed the rewarding sight of the Kilomea flying backward as a heavy slug slammed her in the chest.

Unfortunately, there was an unrewarding sight to counterbalance it as eight more people flowed in through the doors. He called, "Grentham, quit screwing around."

The dwarf replied, "Yeah, yeah." Turrets hidden in the ceiling dropped into view and roared to life, spitting bullets at the newcomers. The invaders reacted by diving into cover and interposing objects lying around in the garage to protect themselves.

Jared snorted. *As if we had enough money to load the turrets with anti-magic rounds. Still, safest play.* He dropped onto his hands and knees and extended his rifle under the car, drawing a breath before pulling the trigger and sliding the weapon from side to side. His rounds were anti-magic, and his enemies hadn't done an adequate job of covering their feet. He managed to drop two before lightning wreathed the SUV and forced him to roll away.

He had a moment of clarity that being proximate to a gasoline-powered vehicle when the enemy had access to magical lightning and fire was a really stupid idea. *Assuming I survive this, I have to think magically more often.* He dashed around the back and ran for the opposite corner, where a small loading area would provide cover.

Grentham copied their foes' tactics to protect him, levitating objects into the path of incoming attacks. His partner called, "Too timid to finish this one-on-one, Angelina?"

She snarled, "Whether it's me or someone else, you'll be just as dead, and I'll be just as happy." Her voice seemed off. Jared peered around the corner and saw her foot was bleeding as she limped toward cover. He lifted his rifle and shot at her but failed to connect.

A heavy tool chest flew at him and forced him to dive aside. He hit the floor awkwardly, wrenching his back. He came up hobbled, unable to straighten, and took stock of the situation.

Grentham managed to intercept all the attacks coming his way, but that left him no opportunity for offense. The one backup person who'd arrived during the fight was already down, and the plan had called for several magicals to be there in support. *Apparently a bit optimistic.* He said, "Might be time to leave, partner."

Grentham replied, "Just a minute or two more. If I can keep them in a stalemate, I'm sure someone will come in on our side."

Jared privately disagreed but deferred to the other man. He drew his pistol and aimed at an enemy who was in between attacks. The anti-magic rounds punched through whatever magical shield she might've had, and she dropped. He hit the catch to release the magazine and reached for a replacement, lifting the gun so it would be easier to slide in the new mag. At that moment, a pair of bullets burned into his torso through the armor gap under his right armpit, killing him.

Grentham heard Jared cry out and twisted in time to see him fall. He reached out with his force magic and grabbed the SUV, sliding it between the attackers and his partner. He ran to Jared's side and knelt beside him, layering force shields around them and nearby, translucent versions that would prevent his enemies from knowing exactly where they were. The other man's eyes were open, but there was no one home. His mouth was parted as if in surprise that someone had shot him.

The advanced trauma kit attached to Jared's thigh emitted the steady sound that everyone who had ever seen a medical show knew meant that his pulse had dropped to zero. The human jerked convulsively as the kit shocked him to try to get his heart working properly again. Nonetheless, the relentless tone continued unchanged. *I can't portal him out of here until the machine does its job. I might mess it up.* In retrospect, Grentham should have learned more about how the medical unit worked, but he never really imagined they'd wind up using it.

Magic slammed into his defenses, and a quick look showed that he had maybe ten seconds before his enemies were in position to shoot through the magical barrier. There was no doubt in his mind that they had anti-magic bullets loaded, enough to put holes in him from head to toe. Finally, the tone changed to beeping, and the man before him gasped. Grentham created a portal underneath them, and they fell through it together.

In the garage, Angelina frowned as the magical defenses suddenly cut off, revealing no one where the dwarf and the downed human had been. She shook her head. "You know, I really figured he'd stick around for a fight to the end."

The Kilomea, wincing as she moved, stepped up beside her. "We'll get them next time."

Angelina sighed. "Maybe we can buy them out. This

whole situation is a distraction we don't need. It will be hard for them to keep operating once we steal all their stuff, which might give us enough leverage to convince them to sell. Is the other thing ready?"

The other woman grinned. "Oh, yeah."

"Let's get it done then."

Twenty minutes later, they'd thoroughly looted the facility, and she was back outside, gazing at the damaged lobby windows. "Blow it." At her command, the signal went out to detonate the satchel charges they'd distributed throughout the structure.

A loud crashing *bang* made her teeth vibrate, and the building shuddered for a moment in a way that rigid structures definitely shouldn't. She watched it collapse in upon itself with immense satisfaction, the perfectly placed explosives leaving nothing higher than a doorway still standing.

Angelina grinned. "Now that's what I call a successful operation. Let's get out of here."

CHAPTER TWENTY-THREE

Elnyier surveyed the concerned faces of the Council members around her. Events on the surface had necessitated a special session. The others were doubtless fearful and irritated, each in their measure. *At the end of the day, they'd prefer a quiet life with prosperous casinos and abundant recreation.*

She kept her expression neutral, but inside, she laughed dismissively. *Small minds, small goals, small dreams. Not like me.* She said, "I think we can assume that Grentham won't be joining us, which means we're all here. Who has useful information about the incident at Aces Security?" She had plenty from a source with first-hand knowledge, but she wasn't interested in sharing it with them.

Bartrak grunted, "Building blew up. Interesting how security companies keep going boom around here."

Anders Caruthers, the wizard, shook his head. "It's nothing to make light of. Beyond the fact that many of us use that company and might now have to deal with service interruptions, it certainly isn't good for the city's reputation to have some bizarre war between corporations."

Rayar, who never failed to annoy her, added, "It does seem quite strange that Aces and Worldspan, assuming that they were the instigators and not only the victims, should turn from profit to combat. I wonder what's going on behind the scenes there."

Elnyier knew. She'd been given notice before the operation as a token of respect from Angelina Prash. Again, she wasn't about to share. Lachsan observed, "Whatever's happening with them, it doesn't really matter to us."

Anders countered, "Easy for you to say since you didn't contract with either of them. I wonder how Challen feels about it."

The gnome blinked, apparently not expecting anyone to call upon him. "The incident at Invention was extremely unfortunate. We're still making repairs. To their credit, Aces had offered to share the expense of doing so since they were responsible for security when the event happened. This event certainly enhances the rumor that the attack on our casino was more about Aces than about us."

Andrielle, the Atlantean, scowled. "Or, maybe it was more of the anti-human nonsense that's been going around. Seriously, that's bad for business. Elnyier, their leader is rumored to be one of your people. Can you talk to him?"

She opened her mouth to give the woman an annoyed response at the insinuation, despite its accuracy, but all that came out was a gasp. The door to the chamber—kept locked during Council meeting— exploded into the room with the broken body of a security guard atop it. Three identically clad figures in tactical clothes and eye masks flowed in afterward, already on the attack.

Bullets flew, accompanied by the chattering of guns, a sound Elnyier had never actually heard in person before. Lachsan, Andrielle, and Anders all spilled out of their chairs, victims of the initial volley. She rose and created a wall of shadow surrounding the Council. More gunfire sounded, and bullets sprayed through her protective shield. Fortunately, Challen and Rayar had ducked, and Bartrak was crouched beneath the line of fire, moving toward the trio.

Rosalind had risen, however, and took a round in the chest that spun her around and dropped her to the floor. Elnyier switched tactics, letting the shield fall and grabbing the table with her force magic. She hurled it at the invaders, right over Bartrak's head, and it forced them to release their weapons and cast spells to stop it.

The fact that it required all three of them to deal with the force she'd put out brought a fierce smile to her face. She followed the table with chairs, a cabinet, everything not bolted down, hoping she'd get lucky and score a hit. The trio stayed clustered, two of them protecting against her further attacks. The third repositioned her rifle, pointing it at the spot where Challen and Rayar huddled over the fallen witch.

The gnome yelled, "We've gotta get out of here," and Rayar replied, "Elnyier, Bartrak, come closer." She complied, but the Kilomea had other plans. He threw himself in the path of the bullets aimed at the trio on the floor, the rounds punching into his heavy vest. The blow staggered him, but he righted himself and rushed forward, causing all three of the attackers to shift their attention to him as the closest threat.

Elnyier spun and ran, passing through the portal Rayar had created. She panted in fear or outrage for a moment, then turned to assist in pulling the witch through. Her last view of the Council chamber showed Bartrak slumping to the floor, perforated by bullets and burned by magical fire.

Rayar closed the portal and stared at her. She stared back, wondering why he had that look on his face. After a short delay, he said, "Elnyier. You need to alert the kemana that we're under attack."

She jolted back to the moment. "Oh, right. Yes." She opened a portal to her underground home, which had duplicates of all the communication options available in the castle, and rushed through. *Right, we'll get this under control first. Then I'm going to find out who those wenches were and where they live. We need to have a conversation about who sent them.*

Two minutes after Ruby had received Morrigan's message, she rushed out of her bedroom with Idryll at her heels. She found her father in the study, sitting in one of the leather chairs with a tumbler of whiskey in his hand. Her mother sat beside him with a matching glass. Normally she was a wine drinker, but apparently, the night's events had rattled her, too. Ruby asked, "What's the situation?"

Rayar shrugged. She noticed he had droplets of blood on his suit, and his hair was far more rumpled than she'd ever seen it after breakfast time. "Rosalind is with Challen. He says she should be fine, that the bullet didn't hit anything vital. Elnyier is off coordinating the response, I guess. I'm sure we'll have a ton of Drow patrolling the streets and guarding the castle in no time."

Ruby blinked in disbelief. "And everyone else?"

Her father sighed and finished the liquid in his glass, then refilled it halfway from the decanter at his side. "Lachsan, Andrielle, and Anders went down right away. Gunfire." He shuddered a little, then continued, "Bartrak intercepted a bunch of bullets meant for Challen and me. I don't think he made it, either."

Grief at the senseless killings and fury at the fact that they had happened in her city filled her. "Who did it? Who were they?"

Sinnia unexpectedly replied, "He said they were three women, all dressed alike, wearing masks."

Her father added, "Different colored hair, though."

Ruby scowled. "I've heard about them. They were involved in the Taka Tower thing. Rumor has it they were helping the PDA with a bounty, going after the city's protectors." Demetrius had acquired that information for her after they'd appeared at that battle.

She sat to avoid pacing, which would lead to gesturing, which would lead to ranting and possibly screaming. With an abundance of calm, she said, "I wonder if Andrews was behind this."

Her mother replied, "Surely he wouldn't stoop so low as to attack the Council."

"I'd like to agree. But times are weird in Magic City, and all his actions suggest he's under some kind of pressure. I have no idea from who." Ruby shook her head. "Okay. Our primary concern is making sure our people keep their eyes open and report anything they see immediately. Can we use one of the numbers at Spirits as an above-ground reporting line and have people contact Matthias here in the kemana?"

Her father waved a hand. "Yes, whatever you need to do. I'll be able to help in just a few minutes once I get a bit steadier." He drank off the rest of his whiskey. "Our world just got exponentially more dangerous, now that our leadership is compromised."

Ruby nodded. "True. But we'll get through it like we always do." *Speaking of compromised, it's time I had a little chat with Elnyier.*

CHAPTER TWENTY-FOUR

The crisis had brought everyone home. Ruby and Morrigan took the lead to make sure their house had protection. It already had detection and security spells all around, but they checked them out one by one to ensure they were still working and fully powered.

Dralen detailed several security guards from Spirits to patrol the area outside their house, claiming not to trust the new Council leader or her people. He got into an argument with Rayar about it, where the pair shouted words like martial law. Ruby wasn't sure if they were talking about Elnyier's actions in the kemana, which admittedly now had a preponderance of Drow in evidence, or the behavior of the PDA above. *One problem at a time.*

When the house was as prepared as it would get, Ruby went up to her room to prepare. She put on the dress she'd worn when she was confirmed as *Mirra*, for the first time wishing she had some sort of ornamentation that would indicate her status. *Yes, I'm legitimate, and you should listen to* me. It's just that my crown melted into my head. I'm sure that'll go over well.

She snorted at her reflection. She was leaving all her normal magical protections behind because someone might've seen them on her costumed alter ego, and she didn't want anyone making that particular connection.

Idryll could travel in public in her true form rather than covered by an illusion that disguised her as a human or Mist Elf. Ruby thought they made an imposing pair. She met her companion's eyes. "Time to throw our weight around. You ready?"

For once, Idryll didn't reply with a quip or an insult. "I am."

Ruby walked at a moderate pace through the kemana, neither trying to draw attention nor seeking to avoid it. The sight of the shapeshifter in her full furry glory was doubtless the reason most people stopped what they were doing to peer at them as they went by, however. Murmurs filled the air.

The Mist Elves they passed touched a knuckle to their forehead in acknowledgment of her status, right where the crown would be if they'd been wearing it. She nodded and smiled at each, every interaction adding another layer of conviction and authority in her mind.

She stopped at the palace door. It was closed, in itself a change from the norm. The guards were both armored in ceremonial garb and armed with long spears. Both were also Drow. "*Mirra* Ruby of the Mist Elves to see Elnyier."

One replied, "The lady is not seeing visitors."

She countered, "The *lady*," she emphasized the title, "will see me, I'm sure. Please announce me."

The one on her right shook his head. The one on the left brought his weapon down in her direction. Before he could finish the action, Idryll had grabbed below the metal part of the spear with one hand and slashed through the wooden haft with the claws of her other.

The second guard jerked as if he would move, and Ruby barked, "Let's not. As I requested, please ask the lady to see me. If she refuses, we'll leave peacefully."

Idryll growled, "But if you try anything like that again, I'm going to take this spear back from you and shove the point of it right down your throat." She tossed the shortened weapon to the stunned guard and resumed her position at Ruby's side.

Ruby whispered, "Way to set off an interspecies incident."

Her companion gave a soft snort. "She should consider upgrading her external defenses to models that have a brain."

Ruby managed not to laugh. A couple of moments later, the doors opened to reveal a guard who beckoned them forward. They exchanged no words as the guard brought them into a small office. Elnyier rose to shake her hand. "*Mirra*. Congratulations on your ascension."

She gestured to the other chair as she sat, and Ruby lowered herself into it. "The Mist Elves see their leader as more servant than deity so ascension might be the wrong word. Nonetheless, thank you for the comment."

Elnyier stilled her face to an expression Ruby recalled having seen her wear before. "So, what is so important that you felt the need to accost my guards?"

Ruby replied calmly, "Actually, it was my companion

who accosted your guards, and they moved first. She is honor-bound to defend me at all costs or avenge me, if necessary." She had no idea if that last part was true, but dang, it sounded good. *Maybe Dad was right, and I do need to throw my weight around a little more often.*

"Semantics. Please, I'm a busy person, as you no doubt are as well. The purpose of your visit?"

Ruby shrugged. "To inform you that the Mist Elves will look out for our interests if needed. We do not cede all authority for defense of the kemana, or the city above, to you. And, if you don't get things together and bring both places under control, you should expect that someone will replace you."

Elnyier laughed. "You believe your father can manage the votes?"

Ruby shrugged again. "I think there are many ways to create an opening at the head of the Council."

The other woman's eyes narrowed. "Did you just threaten me?"

She stood. "No. I asked you to do your job and explained that there will be consequences if you do not. Perhaps you thought that leading the Council would be easy, or enjoyable, or lucrative. Or perhaps it was simply hubris that put you there. In any case, now we must rely on you to fulfill the obligations of the role. If you can't, maybe you should see if Maldren is free."

She could tell she'd irritated the other woman by the way her teeth ground together as she said, "Farewell, *Mirra.*"

Ruby nodded. "You as well, Lady."

After chatting with one of the bees in her bonnet, it was time to deal with the next. Ruby, Morrigan, and Idryll spent a couple of hours setting the stage. Then Ruby snuck into the back of a vehicle Demetrius had unlocked for her to wait.

It didn't take long before Paul Andrews and his second in command, Charlotte Krenn, emerged from the PDA office to head to dinner as they did most nights. When they climbed in the car, Ruby popped up from the backseat, fully costumed and holding one of Margrave's lightning grenades. She'd passed the previous hour thinking through all the potential opening lines she might use, selecting and discarding them one after the other.

Now, at the moment, only one seemed appropriate. She laughed as she tossed the grenade and called up a protective shield around herself. "You guys are so screwed."

When the pair regained consciousness, straps at elbows, wrists, knees, and ankles bound them to simple wooden chairs. Ruby and her partners had gagged the agents because Ruby wanted a chance to say what she'd come to say without being interrupted. She slapped each of them a few times to make sure they were fully awake. *I might have hit Andrews a little harder than strictly necessary, but I think he's earned it.*

She crouched so her dragon mask was eye-to-eye with the PDA director. "So, we meet again." He tried to talk through the gag, and she slapped him again, gently this time. "No, no. You're going to listen for a while. I'm sure you have a locator, and I'm sure people are on their way, but we'll be gone before they get here."

When she said "we," his eyes started frantically looking around. Ruby laughed. "Oh yes, my partners are here, too. One has an incendiary arrow ready to go. You may have noticed that everything in here is old wood, and this warehouse is in a location where it won't damage anything else if it burns down. So, behave, please."

She prowled around the captive pair, letting the tension build. "We tried this the nice way. You responded by sending bounty hunters after us." There were muffled shouts, and she shook her head. "Don't try to deny it because I won't believe you. It takes someone like you, someone who knows the system, to so blatantly misuse it.

"You put a fake bounty on us, which attracted some hunters. You should consider yourself lucky you only listed us as a level one, or you might've ticked me off." The way he'd worked the system still made her furious whenever she thought of it.

"We've eliminated those false records, by the way. If you try it again, well, let's just say you *shouldn't* try it again, or evidence of your tampering will reach those above you. But let me get back to what I was saying. So, the bounty hunters you brought to town then tried to kill the Council."

Andrews struggled, and his muffled words grew more frantic. Ruby sighed. "The part where I said you need to shut up and listen? That's a real thing. Shut the hell up."

She pushed her irritation away and continued speaking. "I don't think you sent them after the Council. That would be incredibly stupid, and while you're overly aggressive, disrespectful of people's rights, generally a scumbag, and have dramatically questionable taste in cologne, one thing you aren't is stupid.

"So, either someone's trying to frame you and get the PDA in trouble with Magic City above and below the surface, or someone took advantage of the situation and hired them for a different gig. Or both. I suppose the reason behind the action really doesn't matter. The result is pretty clear." She used magic to rip off his gag and asked the director, "So, am I right?"

He scowled and worked his jaw for a moment. "I won't confirm anything you said, but we had nothing to do with the attack on the Council. You're correct. That would be the height of stupidity. Hell, I wanted the Council to help with things on the surface and told them so."

She laughed. "You may find that people in town don't trust you all that much. I wonder why that is." She walked around and removed the woman's gag as well.

Krenn didn't speak, only stared daggers at her. Ruby patted her on the shoulder. "I know. I'm sorry his actions inconvenienced you. Still, you chose to work where you work, so you have only yourself to blame."

She circled back to Andrews. "I want to make sure we understand each other. From here on out, if you act against me and mine in any way, I won't hurt your people. I won't harm you physically. But I will burn your career to the ground.

"Rest assured that I have the resources and the connections to do it. Your decision to mess with the Ely PD's systems gave me all the evidence I need. So, do your job properly, without all the Gestapo tactics, and we'll be cool.

"Fail to do that, and your second here is going to get a promotion. Then I'll have this conversation again with her. Although maybe with the fire already going as an incentive."

Ruby put her hands on her hips and cocked her head to the side. "The real question is whether we give you that chance or burn you down here and now." She raised her voice. "What do you guys think?"

Idryll replied, "Fire. Fire is good. I brought marshmallows." Andrews and his sidekick started to struggle, probably a reflexive reaction.

Morrigan said, "No. I don't want to waste the arrow. Then I'd have to take, like, fifteen minutes to make another one. It'd be a whole thing. Let's just go. Besides, his friends are inbound. He'd likely only end up getting singed, anyway."

Ruby nodded. "You got off lucky this time, Paulie. Make sure we don't have to do this again." She strode out of their lines of sight into the darkness of the warehouse and portaled back to the bunker. *Right, that's two problems down. Now I need to take care of some internal business.*

CHAPTER TWENTY-FIVE

Ruby met Diana in front of Shentia's shop as the agent stepped out and closed the door behind her. The other woman said, "Running errands for Nylotte, of course. You'd think at some point I'd be done with that, but no, apparently not."

She laughed. "I owe Shentia a whole bunch of tasks, so I know exactly what you mean."

It seemed odd now to see the agent without her almost ever-present sidekick, Rath. *But it could be this isn't something he'd fully understand.* Ruby had asked Diana for advice on her current life situation, and Diana had decided it would be best to include her mentor in that conversation. *Or maybe she knows he'd be bored.* The agent created a portal connecting the two kemanas, and they stepped through to Stonesreach, the one underneath the city of Pittsburgh.

Diana opened the door of Nylotte's business, which on the outside largely resembled Shentia's. Inside, things were a little different. Nylotte's place held fewer items, and the objects there seemed more elegant, or more expensive, or more rare. Or, in many cases, all three. The Drow was seated behind the counter that separated her from her clients. "Diana. Ruby. Welcome."

Diana replied, "Thanks for agreeing to join us on this."

Nylotte shrugged. "Always glad to be of assistance."

Ruby wondered what the woman's involvement would wind up costing her. *I've got part of an arm I might be willing to give up. Stupid artifact.* She asked, "So, are we going to talk here?"

The Drow chuckled. "Eager, are we? Actually, I think this would be an excellent moment for tea."

She stood and brushed by them on her way to the door, and they followed her outside. Ruby exchanged a glance with Diana, but the agent only shrugged. Nylotte led them to a modest restaurant, where the proprietor, another Drow, escorted them to a small loft. It held four tables, none occupied, and they selected the one in the farthest back corner.

Nylotte filled the time with light conversation until their tea arrived, and they all took an appreciative sip in silence. Finally, she nodded. "Okay, now that our minds and spirits are at ease, speak."

Ruby replied, "I have a couple of questions. First, you may have heard I'm now the leader of the Mist Elves." Both women shook their heads, and she laughed. "Well, I guess it's fair to say it's more notable if you're a Mist Elf. Nonetheless, I am."

Nylotte frowned and looked at Diana. "Wasn't the last girl you were involved with, Kelly or whatever, some kind of leader, too?"

The agent rolled her eyes. "Please. You don't forget

anything. It's Cali, and yes, though not of a whole magical group."

The Drow turned back to her, and Ruby decided the woman had commented to ensure she didn't get too big a head about her new position. Nylotte asked, "So what's the issue?"

Ruby drew a deep breath. "Between the two of you, you have a lot of experience leading and mentoring. I wondered if you have any pointers to share."

Nylotte lifted an eyebrow. "If you have to ask that question, you're not ready."

Diana sighed and shook her head. "Honestly, you're in a snit today, aren't you?" She reached over and gripped Ruby's arm briefly.

"Based on my experience with you, you'll do fine, regardless of what sourpuss there says. Long story short, you can only make decisions with the knowledge you have, so do your best to ensure new information is always flowing in from as diverse a set of sources as possible. Beyond that, be kind when you're able, hard when you have to, and as even-handed and consistent as circumstances allow."

The advice helped Ruby release some tension. "It's good to hear that since I was sort of already thinking along those lines. I'll try to make sure I do that."

Diana replied, "You'll do great. Seriously. Don't stress about it. What's the other thing?"

Ruby absently rubbed her arm. "I think you both know I'm the reluctant owner of a Rhazdon artifact. In the inner space where I talk to my sword, I can also talk to the artifact. It offered to train me to cast spells through the sword.

Says it can do so much more effectively and efficiently than anyplace else I might get that knowledge."

Nylotte frowned. "Does it now? Seems strange that the entity in the sword hasn't done that for you."

"Entities," Ruby specified. "They didn't believe it was possible. Apparently, in this, the Atlantean has knowledge they do not."

Diana asked, "The Atlantean?"

Ruby waved a hand. "The representation of the artifact in my head is an Atlantean man. He's a jerk."

Nylotte replied, "Kelly's Atlantean."

Diana sighed. "*Cali*. Sometimes it's hard to tell if you're getting meaner or just senile. Anyway, I don't think what form the artifact chooses as its avatar is a vital concern. Do you have any other way to learn this information?"

Ruby shrugged. "My mentor on Oriceran doesn't have that skill, as far as I know. Certainly, she's neither shown that ability during our bouts nor offered to teach me."

Nylotte replied, "Not every artifact can do it, and not everyone who uses an artifact can, either. It requires a deep level of synergy between the wielder and the weapon."

Ruby frowned. "Does that mean I'll be risking a deeper connection with the Rhazdon artifact, too?"

The Drow looked thoughtful. "It's entirely possible. I couldn't say for certain, as this isn't something I've had personal experience with before."

Diana said, "I understand how important being able to do this would be for your fighting style. That certainly adds weight to one side of the scale."

Ruby's head bobbed. "Very much so."

Nylotte commented, "I could potentially teach you, but

I couldn't do it quickly. I would have to spend substantial time communing with the personalities in your sword and adapting to them before I'd know exactly how to guide you to the appropriate connection."

Diana replied, "Which the artifact has likely already done, giving it an advantage."

Ruby said, "You seem to think it's a good idea."

The agent shrugged. "It would be a useful skill for you to have. If that's the only way to get it in a reasonable timeframe, then the answer becomes kind of obvious."

She drew a deep breath, then released slowly. "If I decide to do it, do you have any suggestions about how?"

Diana nodded. "Definitely. Do it here."

An hour later, Ruby was kneeling in the centermost ring of Nylotte's circle of wards. She had already descended from the outermost portion of her mind to a meditative space and was ready to move on. Diana said, sounding like she was speaking from a long distance away, "If you need anything, we're here."

Since the problem is my brain, I'm not sure what all you can do from there. "Thanks. Here goes nothing."

She placed her hand on the artifact, and it squirmed under her touch. Fighting down nausea, she imagined her rug and chairs in the grassland expanse and tried to will herself to go there. Instead, her perceptions shifted, and she found herself on a landscape full of sharp-edged formations and painted in harsh colors. A hot wind whipped through the space, and the Atlantean stepped into view. He said, "So you decided to accept my training. Smart girl."

"Let's get one thing straight. I'm in charge here."

He laughed. "Oh, of course."

She scowled. "No, I mean it. Any games and I might have to find out if cutting off a limb can truly free one of a Rhazdon artifact."

He replied dismissively, "Others have tried. Didn't work."

"Like I'd believe you on that matter."

The Atlantean nodded. "So you *can* learn, excellent. Let's begin. Bring yourself into a fighting stance." She complied. He continued, "Imagine the sword in your hands." She did as he asked and felt the cold metal of the hilt pressing into her skin.

"It's a simple mental shift. Right now, you cast with your hands, your voice, your body. The key is imagining the weapon is as seamlessly you as those things are. It stands to reason that if the sword is merely another body part, you can cast magic through it."

Ruby replied, "It's that easy?"

"To find the starting point, yes. To achieve the necessary connection, less so. But I am prepared to guide you once you begin."

She drew a deep breath and blew it out. "Okay, I'll try." She imagined the sword as an extension of her arm and considered what it would be like to feel the magic spreading from her hand into the weapon.

Ruby focused on visualizing that feeling, making it as real as she could in her mind. She was uncharacteristically patient with herself, letting the image build at its own pace.

When she found blockages barring her way, the Atlantean gave her advice, and she moved gently around them to find new paths.

In the end, Ruby felt like she had made progress, maybe even succeeded. Maintaining the idea of her sword as an extension of her arm had become, if not easy, then not incredibly complicated, either. She said, "I'll have to try this outside, of course."

"Naturally."

"Thank you for your help." She returned to the real world, where her sword lay on her palms. She concentrated on it while also sending her thoughts toward its inhabitants, asking for their help. After a moment of intense visualization of the weapon as an extension of her body, it began to glow softly.

Diana clapped, and Nylotte said, "Well done, Ruby. It will take more practice and more effort to make it part of your arsenal, but you've taken an important first step."

She rose and nodded, but inside she groaned. *Where am I going to find time for* more *training?*

CHAPTER TWENTY-SIX

After returning from her meeting-turned-training-session with Diana and Nylotte, Ruby decided the status quo couldn't be allowed to stand any longer. She summoned Morrigan and Idryll to the bunker, and they gathered in the living room. The other two sat, but she was too keyed up for immobility.

She paced as she laid it out for them. "Okay, even after our intervention with Andrews, he'll still use the Drow as an excuse to hinder us. It gives him the greatest amount of cover and deniability if we make good on our threat to go to his higher-ups."

Idryll asked, "Why threaten? Why not just do it?"

Ruby sighed. "The thing is, while I don't like him personally and I think he made some bad choices professionally, Andrews is fundamentally on the same side we are. At Taka Tower, he made the call to redirect his resources toward the real threat rather than us. So, except as a true last resort, I wouldn't feel right burning him. Literally or figuratively."

Idryll grunted. "I don't have a problem with it."

Morrigan shook her head. "I'm with Ruby on this one. He's a scumbag, but not fundamentally bad. Maybe the hard reset we gave him will help."

Ruby continued, "So, he's one nexus of problems, and we've done what we can with him. Elnyier is another, and hopefully, the visit from the *Mirra* will make a difference. I doubt it, but at least there's a line in the sand that she has to consider now. That leaves our other nexus of problems, the hat-wearing Drow."

Idryll said, "When he goes down, I get the hat. I'd look great in it."

Morrigan laughed, and Ruby replied, "Done deal. Taking him out serves multiple purposes. It gives Andrews less excuse to mess with us, damages Elnyier's aspirations if she's using his actions to influence the Council, and, oh yeah, by the way, protects everyone in Magic City from the chaos he sows. Time to quit reacting and start acting."

Morrigan asked, "How do we find him?"

"Demetrius has been working on that problem and is pretty sure he has a solution for us. Or, more specifically, he'll have one sometime this evening."

Magic spilled out of the receiving room, and Margrave stepped in to join them. "Howdy, neighbors. I bring toys."

They accepted reloads for the items they'd expended in the battle at Taka Tower. He also handed over a thin rectangular container holding five darts, with a slide on either side of the case. He said, "Left-hand slide deploys them one by one. You have to redo it for each dart. Right-hand one pops them all up at once, in a declining pattern.

The change allowed me to make the case smaller, and it will be a lot easier to get a grip on the darts."

Ruby accepted it and admired the craftsmanship. "You do good work, my friend. And I'm sorry to say we need a restock on pretty much everything. We're out of backups."

Margrave shook his head with a laugh. "Expensive business you're in, this defending the city stuff."

She sighed. "Yeah, tell me about it. I'm pretty sure I owe Shentia about a year of my life at this point." He laughed, and she continued, "I'll get some money thrown your way. Not sure how. Maybe I'll embezzle some from Morrigan's bank account."

Her sister warned, "Try it, and I'll visit powerful vengeance upon you. Hack Dralen's instead."

Ruby grinned. "I figured we'd already drained his accounts. Sure, we can take whatever's left."

They joked for a few minutes more, then Demetrius's voice came over her comm. "I've got them."

She, Idryll, and Morrigan instantly sobered, and Margrave looked confused by the change. She explained, "We just got the call. Time to head out to work."

He nodded. "I'll leave you to it and get started on that resupply." He left quietly, and the trio moved into the arming room.

Ruby said, "Don't cut any corners. This one's going to be tough."

She pulled on her base layer, zipped it up, and used donning of each additional item to still her mind and focus her will on the night to come. Physical defense came first, in the form of her heavy boots, her vest, and lightweight armor plates over her shins. She'd been using that part of her body often to block and strike with, and the loss of a tiny amount of speed was a good exchange for reducing the pain of the frequent impacts.

Magical defenses came next. She slipped on her fully recharged shield bracelets, added her shield and illusion pendants, and slid healing flasks into her belt and vest. As usual, she wore a healing capsule and energy capsule underneath her clothes. By the time she completed her defenses, she'd eliminated almost all concerns other than dealing with the Drow and his people.

Then it was time for offense. Ruby checked to ensure the throwing daggers hadn't magically vanished from her boots and reached to pat her wrist dagger, only belatedly remembering she'd returned it to Shentia. She touched the pistol in the holster on that hip instead. She didn't need to check that its loadout held anti-magic bullets. She'd cleaned and readied the weapon earlier in the day, doing the same for Morrigan's gun.

The EMP snapped into a holder on her belt, and she touched each of her grenades in turn, reminding herself of their positions. It wasn't hard since she kept the explosives to the left of the belt buckle, lightning to the right, and the flash-bangs on the left side of her lower back.

The spare darts went on her left side as well because she would need to pull them out with her right hand now that the dart gun was on her left forearm. Next, she slipped the stun knuckles onto her right hand. Finally, she slid into her sword harness and reached back to check the draw. Shalia and Tyrsh touched her mind as her hand gripped the hilt, signaling their readiness to assist. She completed her preparations by slipping on her mask. "I'm ready."

Morrigan said, "Me too."

Idryll sighed loudly. "All those movies where it takes women forever to get dressed? I understand that now. Can we get a move on?"

Instead of replying, Morrigan opened a portal. She said, "D told me where we're heading. This will put us about a block away."

Ruby replied, "Outstanding. Let's do it."

They stepped through to another part of the city. She had no real idea where they were. The rooftop offered no obvious landmarks other than the light spilling into the sky from the Strip in the distance. Morrigan led the way to the other end of the building and pointed at the warehouse across the street. "He says that's the one."

Ruby asked, "Tree, how sure are you of this? How did you figure it out?"

Her boyfriend's response was uncharacteristically subdued. "I called in a favor to refine the triangulation algorithm and applied it to all sightings of the anti-human movement group. Cross-indexing that by time taken to travel, I wound up with three general zones where they could be based.

"I pulled down all the information I could get from PDA drones that had surveyed those areas. That narrowed it further, and I put up some of my drones to watch. They spotted a bunch of people going in there, and they're definitely not warehouse workers. I'm highly confident that's their operating base. Or it's empty and is simply a portal spot."

Ruby replied, "Good enough for me." Morrigan opened a portal so they could step through to the other building, and they scouted the rooftop warily under their veils, looking for surveillance or traps. They found none and advanced to the centermost of the five skylights positioned equidistantly across the structure. A couple of dozen people were inside, not engaged in any particular activity. Ruby said, "Looks like we got to them before they started whatever adventure they have planned for the night."

Idryll remarked, "Too bad for them."

Morrigan asked, "We going in quiet, or we going in loud?"

Ruby replied, "A little of both. We're going in *smart*. Idryll, open the skylight without breaking it, please."

The shapeshifter muttered something that sounded like an insult as she complied. Ruby dropped in all three of her lightning grenades, followed by a couple of flash-bangs. Morrigan, on the opposite side of the opening, dispatched her gas and sonic arrows. Idryll asked, "Are you finished?"

Ruby nodded. "Go for it."

The shapeshifter grinned and jumped through the opening. Morrigan said, "She's a maniac."

"Right?"

As Ruby followed Idryll down, her sister's voice observed, "Perfect companion for you, then. You're both nuts."

She landed on a blast of force to kill her velocity and replied, "Well, you're with us voluntarily, so doesn't that make you crazy, too?"

Morrigan replied, "No, just stupid."

She grinned, amused by her sister's words and the

chaos of the people running around in reaction to their sneak attack. "So, same as always then." One of the Drow's gang noticed her and shouted, and her grin turned to a look of quiet determination. "All right. Stay nonfatal, be safe, knock out the opposition, and find the leader. Go to it."

CHAPTER TWENTY-SEVEN

Morrigan descended slowly into the space, the grapnel on her belt suspending her in midair after a few seconds. The initial barrage had taken out about a third of the group, but they were still notably outnumbered. She drew and fired her flash-bang arrow at a cluster in the corner that seemed like they were getting organized. Her targets stumbled away from the cacophony, cursing and moaning.

She selected a razor arrow and put it through the leg of a motionless Kilomea crouched behind a forklift, who was waiting for Idryll to draw near enough for him to pounce. Confidence in her accuracy had returned in full, and she felt the likelihood of a fatal wound was minimal. *I'll do my best, but that means taking easy shots as they present themselves, too. Dropping him early ensures I don't have to risk a reaction shot at him later.* She was aware her thoughts amounted to justification rather than deliberation, but she was good with that.

A burst of flame rose at an angle. Morrigan slapped the button to release the grapnel, falling the rest of the way to the floor to avoid the fireball and landing on a blast of force magic.

She smoothly drew and fired an arrow at the elf who'd tried to burn her, but he waved a hand, and her projectile veered harmlessly to the side. She sent another on a slower arc, knowing he'd do the same again but using his distraction as an opportunity to close. Her bow transformed into a baton, and she shoved it into the holster on her thigh.

By the time she reached the elf, her daggers were in her hands. She attacked him as she arrived, not allowing him enough time to marshal magic defenses. He slapped at her hands ineffectively, apparently entirely reliant on his magic.

She sliced him several times in the initial flurry, which discomfited him sufficiently that when he raised his hands to summon a spell, it failed to materialize. Morrigan lashed out with her foot, slamming him in the groin, and he crumpled. "Idiot." She summoned a veil and ran for cover, sheathing her daggers and retrieving her bow on the way.

Idryll reveled in the freedom to lay into the surrounding enemies. The battle at Taka Tower had been frustrating on several levels. It had been evident to her they had no chance of adequately defending the building, so their main objective was out of reach from the start. Then the Drow's swords had proven too much for her defenses. She had a plan for that if she met him again, and she intensely hoped that opportunity would materialize.

In the meantime, taking out his minions was deeply

pleasurable. She used her natural agility to great advantage, sliding out of the way of attacks, shifting from one opponent to the next to sow confusion and create targeting challenges, and slicing with her claws at areas that would cause pain and distraction rather than lasting damage. She'd partially transformed to increase her speed and strength, and already several opponents were down.

A Kilomea caught her with one of the pair of axes he wielded and knocked her off balance to slam into a nearby wall. He advanced quickly, weaving the blades through a defensive pattern that showed his mastery of them. He'd struck her with the flat part of the weapon, her last-minute twist allowing her to avoid the edge, so the wound was more to her pride than to her body.

She strode forward to meet him, increasing her transformation to strengthen her muscles further. She loved fighting the giant creatures and considered them a worthy rival in a way that most other magicals and humans weren't.

The Kilomea recognized her as a threat. His approach turned cautious, and he was careful not to overreach as he sliced at her with the axes. She batted the first blows aside contemptuously, her speed now near its maximum potential. The blocks left an opening, and she slid in and slammed his chest with her shoulder, knocking him back a couple of steps. He stepped forward and wrapped his arms around her in a bear hug, with her body still perpendicular to his.

He smashed his forehead in at her ear, and she jerked her head away in time to take the brunt of the impact on her collarbone. It withstood the blow without cracking, something she was sure it wouldn't have done in her normal humanoid form. She couldn't move a lot, but he'd foolishly left a vulnerable spot unprotected.

She whipped a quick hammer fist into his groin, then snarled in frustration as it impacted some sort of metal armor. The Kilomea laughed and squeezed harder. Idryll found his grin entirely annoying. "As much as I'd like to play with you, I don't have the time right now."

She transformed into a tiger, jumped up, and turned in the small amount of free space the shape change provided. All four sets of claws raked her foe. He fell back with a harsh bellow of pain, and she twisted to land on her feet.

The mask on its elastic strap was still in place, and her equipment belt had released when she transformed. She leapt at him, and he dropped onto his back to allow her to pass overhead, lifting both axes so she'd slice herself on them as she crossed.

A quick change into her house cat form carried her up and over the weapons, the momentum of her bigger body easily sending her smaller one higher and farther. She was back in tiger form by the time she landed and spun to charge him. He tried to scramble to his feet, but she caught him in the middle of his rise and slammed bodily into him.

He crashed against the wall with the sound of at least one breaking bone, and she raced forward to bite the forearm of the hand that still held a weapon. She savaged the limb, wrenching it back and forth, cutting muscles and tendons. When she finished, he was clearly out of the fight.

Idryll transformed back into her humanoid form, secured her fallen mask and equipment belt, and threw the medical pouch from her belt down to the wounded Kilomea. "Better stop the bleeding, or you won't be around to see how your gang crumbles."

Ruby focused on fighting with her sword, using her off-hand alternately to shield and cast offensive magic. She was careful to strike with the flat of the blade and to cut in nonfatal areas. It was a difficult line to walk, given how many enemies were present. Some of those who'd gone down in the initial barrage were climbing back to their feet, and she hoped they'd have the good sense to run rather than continue to fight.

That thought led to another. "We need to keep a few of these jerks around for questioning. I haven't seen the leader, have you?" The others replied in the negative, and Ruby shook her head. "Maybe one of these chuckleheads knows where he is. We have to finish them fast."

Morrigan replied, "On it."

Idryll said, "Less talking, more fighting, fearless leader."

Ruby snorted and took down a dwarf with a blast of force magic that smashed him into the gnome next to him. While they were both dazed, she tapped them with the stun knuckles, knocking them out. She'd already expended three darts and fired two more in rapid succession at an approaching Kilomea. He managed to deflect the first with his giant club—*is that a cricket bat?*—but the second lodged in his cheek. He looked annoyed, then confused, and fell.

She cast a veil and ran for cover, then hit the slide to pop up her reloads. She inserted them into the dart gun's chambers through the cleverly hinged back that allowed the dart to slide through in one direction but prevented it from slipping back out afterward. *Margrave, you're a genius.*

A body bumped into her back, and she spun to exchange blows with an angry-faced female elf. *She looks like a true believer to me, unlike a lot of these folks.* Ruby hit her in the face with a back fist, then kicked her legs out from underneath her, causing her to drop the large knife she'd gripped. A dart into her bare arm sent the elf off to dreamland.

A blast of fire washed over her, and she turned toward the source. Her shields held against the magic, and when it stopped, she was entirely shocked to see her roommate, Shiannor, standing in front of her.

She redirected her reflexive sword slash so it would miss him, then nailed him with a dart as well. She didn't have time to wonder at his presence there, other than to think that maybe the elf chick she'd dropped just before had been the mysterious girlfriend Liam had mentioned. *I can't imagine another explanation for his being here unless he's been completely dishonest about who he is.*

She and her team fought for several more minutes, making sure they had subdued everyone who wasn't smart enough to run away. Finally, about a dozen of the Drow's minions were seated or lying in a circle, back to back, and Morrigan was above on overwatch with an arrow nocked. Ruby explained that anyone who even thought about standing would wind up dead from the sudden manifestation of an arrowhead in a vital location, and the fight went out of their opponents.

She kicked a dwarf in the foot. "Hey, where's your boss?" He swore at her, and Ruby sighed. Idryll tried another with no more success. Then Ruby had a thought. "Kitty cat, drag one over to that corner and see if you can persuade him to talk. I'll take this one and do the same." She grabbed Shiannor by his shirt, dragged him to his feet, and threw him toward the opposite side of the warehouse.

He took a clumsy swing at her as they neared their destination. She ducked it and pushed him hard enough that he slammed back against the wall with a groan. *Sorry, Shia, but you put yourself into this situation voluntarily.*

She got right up in his face and growled hoarsely, "I recognize you. You're the one I've seen at the Grinding Axes with the dwarf and the witch. I wonder if your friends over there on the ground know you hang out with a human voluntarily. I wonder what they'd do to you and your bar friends if they found out."

He paled, and his eyes shifted to the group Morrigan was guarding. Ruby wondered if he was looking at his girlfriend but didn't glance over to check. "You have two options. Option one, you go to jail, where the dwarf, the witch, the human, and the other guy that hangs out with you will join you. Accomplices, people of interest, whatever. Their lives will never be the same, and it will be all your fault."

His cringe was satisfying. She continued, "Or, you tell me where your boss is, and you maybe manage to escape from here before the sheriff arrives to arrest you and your friends. Your choice, make it right now."

Shiannor's face crumpled as she watched. "He left just before you got here. Headed for Darkest Night."

She patted him on the shoulder. "Good choice. Don't let

me find you hanging with this crowd again, or it'll be option one."

Morrigan, who'd been listening in over the comm, said, "Well, now we're screwed. We can't barrel into a casino like this."

Ruby ran over, launched Idryll up when the tiger-woman joined her, then force-boosted herself up through the skylight to land cleanly on the roof. "Believe it or not, I have a plan."

CHAPTER TWENTY-EIGHT

It felt weird walking into the Darkest Night casino wearing her natural Mist Elf features. She'd returned to the bunker to quick-change, throwing on the jeans and t-shirt she'd worn earlier in the day, and carried only her purse, which held nothing suspicious. Her sole magic item was the illusion pendant she'd always worn to help with her human disguise, which had proven to be virtually undetectable. The others had argued against the plan, but they couldn't enter in costume, and her sister was immediately recognizable.

She had little doubt that the magic sensors at the casino entrance would be able to detect a complex disguise since security had been upgraded yet again in most of the casinos. So, the least detectable option was Ruby in her true form. She detoured into the restroom and emerged in the Mist Elf persona she used with the biker gang in place of her natural features.

No one outside the Desert Ghosts and the abbey knew that person, and she didn't imagine those folks would overlap much with the casino crowd. A couple of Drow were part of the group, but she couldn't worry about every possible problem, or she'd be unable to act at all.

She walked the floor with a purpose, looking for her target's telltale hat, the only thing that would allow her to spot him from a distance in the sea of Dark Elves that filled the casino. Other magicals were present, naturally, and even some humans milled about, but probably half were of the species that owned the casino.

It was easy to understand the appeal of the place. The false night sky was gorgeous, and the images set into it invoked fear at a visceral level. She found it enthralling and was sure everyone else did, too. Darkest Night had been one of her favorite casinos before the leader of the anti-human movement and the new head of the Council had soured her on Dark Elves. She tried not to judge the many by the few, but it was difficult when the few were so problematic.

She carefully avoided the tables with anti-magic emitters as she circulated, afraid of revealing her disguise. It took fifteen minutes of searching, but finally, she found him headed toward the casino's second floor. She made a beeline to his location and "accidentally" bumped into him, sliding a locator she'd hidden under her purse strap beneath the lapel of his jacket. She apologized in a tumble of words. "Sorry, totally my fault. I'm a little tipsy."

He stared down at her and growled, "Clumsy. Be better."

She apologized again and turned, orienting herself on the exit doors and weaving in that direction. She made it about ten steps before a trio of security guards blocked her path. The meanest-looking one directed, "Come with us, please, ma'am."

Ruby considered fighting her way out, but the odds against her were too great. Unless it was life or death, she had to continue pretending to be an average everyday Mist Elf without much going on inside her head. *No problem, I'll just try to be like Morrigan.*

They escorted her to a small room in the backstage portion of the casino. She noted cameras along the way and further noted that the room they'd entered didn't seem to have one. It was a featureless chamber, with white walls, magical lighting in the corners, and a single metal chair in the center. "Sit," the guard ordered, and she complied without argument.

A few minutes later, the door opened, and a severe-looking Drow in a perfectly tailored suit walked in. The woman had long white hair bound into a ponytail and secured with a series of jeweled bands. It came down over her shoulder and lay on her chest until she tossed it back out of the way and stepped forward toward Ruby.

She made a show of slipping on a leather glove and unceremoniously slapped Ruby across the face with it. "Who are you, and why were you following that person?"

Ruby worked her jaw. *Wench hits hard.* Her lip felt like it was swelling already. "I wasn't." The lie earned her a backhand blow, snapping her head in the opposite direction. "Ouch. Cut it out."

The Drow chuckled. "You're a very poor liar. Why were you following him?"

She looked up at the woman, restraining herself from counterattacking. Taking her assailant would be easy.

Managing to get all three of the other guards holding positions on different walls before they could call for assistance would be less so. *This explains the lack of cameras in the room.* She replied, "Seriously. It's only a coincidence."

The Drow muttered and waved her hand, and Ruby suddenly felt like small creatures were chewing on every inch of her skin. She stiffened in the chair and forced herself to remain immobile as the pain increased. The torment lasted for ten seconds, at the end of which she was about ready to scream.

It vanished as quickly as it had appeared. Her tormentor said, "Last chance. Lie to me again, and you'll get more of what you just had, say, an hour or so. You'll be a babbling idiot by the time it's over."

Ruby sighed and tried to look both guilty and superficial. "Okay. Fine. This is really embarrassing. You're right. I *was* following him. I saw him and thought he was super sexy, especially with the hat. I only wanted to make a connection. But when I bumped into him, he looked at me like I was dirt. So, I needed to get out of there before I said something stupid."

The Drow slapped her across the face again, the leather glove raising a welt. "Moron. He's out of your league. Plus, he's taken." The woman looked at the guards. "I think we've got the truth now. Find anything in her bag?"

The guard holding it shook his head. "Only the normal stuff." *Thank goodness I left everything except my illusion pendant at home.*

Her tormentor nodded. "Okay. Throw her out."

They did so, quite literally, and she received a solid scrape on one hand from the pavement. She kept up the disguise until she was out of sight of the casino, then portaled to the bunker. She stomped into the arming room and started putting on her fighting gear. When she slipped on her comm and reported she was back, Morrigan asked, "Are you okay?"

Ruby growled, "Fine. Do we have him?"

Demetrius replied, "Yep. He's left the casino and is walking back toward the warehouse. By now, he has to know you all were there messing up his gang."

Ruby said, "Okay. Idryll, stay with him. Morrigan, come get me." Ruby's portaling had improved drastically of late, but she didn't reliably have her sister's pinpoint accuracy. This was one time where she couldn't afford to be off. A few minutes later, the trio was together again, paralleling the Drow's path on the rooftops.

He headed into a convenience store. Her sister asked, "Wait for him?"

Ruby shook her head and leapt from the building to the ground. "No. For all we know, he'll portal out of there, and we'll lose him again. He probably has more than one coat, so we can't trust the tracker to be able to pick him up later. Let's go nail him now."

They adopted their usual normal person disguises and entered the store. Their target was standing near the register, chatting with the cashier. A fancy cold coffee drink sat before him on the counter. The three of them separated to examine the shelves and position themselves to act. Ruby whispered, "Morrigan, get a portal to the receiving room ready. I'll tackle him through it, and we'll deal with him there."

"On it."

It took them a few seconds to get properly positioned. Ruby said, "Do it," and rushed toward him. When she reached the point where her body should've contacted his, she realized he wasn't really there. It was only a very convincing illusion. Morrigan dispelled the portal before Ruby stumbled through it, and they looked around in surprise.

The Drow reappeared in the corner behind the cashier, laughing. "So nice of you to come. I figured at least one of you would be watching for me at Darkest Night after my gang told you I was there. Sorry your little game didn't work." He shook his head sadly. "Pity for you, really. Especially since *my* plan worked perfectly."

With the ripple of magic, Dante's Angels appeared, one near each of them, and attacked.

CHAPTER TWENTY-NINE

The reversal was one step too far for Ruby. Anger burst out of her in a scream as she sent a force blast at the Drow to distract him. She grabbed the shelving unit nearest the blonde Angel and yanked, smashing it into her and sending her rifle shots into the ceiling.

Morrigan had raced for cover ahead of the line of bullets that sought her. Idryll had simply performed a somersault over the nearest set of shelves to break the line of sight with her attacker. *So everyone's okay, for the moment.*

The collapsed shelf flew to the side to reveal the bounty hunter. Ruby reached out with her force magic, grabbed the rifle, and yanked. Her opponent jerked forward before the strap broke, and Ruby hurled the weapon through the glass window at the front of the store, shattering it. Her mind had entered an unfamiliar space where the consequences of her actions, normally in the center of her thoughts, were muffled and distant.

The Drow drew his swords, and Ruby growled, "No way." She spun to face the opposite direction, drawing her sword in her right hand and angling it toward him. She extended her left at the blonde Angel with the intent of shooting her with the dart gun. Instead, shadow tentacles erupted from the artifact and reached out to cover the woman. Her foe screamed as the magic burned into the exposed flesh of her face.

Ruby grinned coldly. "Serves you right, wench." She turned her attention to the Drow, who was advancing far more cautiously now. She quipped, "Are you afraid, little elf? Come a bit closer, and I'll drive all worries out of your mind." *By stabbing them with a foot of magical steel.*

Morrigan's initial reaction had been to go for her bow, but the confined space argued against it. Instead, she drew her daggers and faced off against the redhead Angel. A crescent kick knocked the rifle out of her foe's hands, and rather than trying to regain it, her opponent went for her pistols. Morrigan tossed her left-hand dagger in the air and blasted the other woman with lightning.

The bounty hunter flew into the glass door of a soda cooler, shattering it. Morrigan caught her dagger as the Angel rebounded fighting, summoning a protective force shield over each fist and throwing a punch at her face. She yanked her head backward to avoid it and backpedaled as the other woman threw more kicks and blows at her.

Morrigan had a good sense of her location in the place, and before reaching the point where a wall at her back would force her to counter, she stepped into the woman's attack. Her daggers stabbed into her foe's biceps, lacking power but still penetrating. Morrigan released them and punched the Angel's throat, meeting a protective armor collar. Her jab at the woman's ribs hit her vest, rendering it ineffective as well.

Her opponent cried out, probably more in anger than pain, and smashed her hands inward at Morrigan's head. She threw herself back and down, bringing her foot up under the Angel's chin. The kick connected, and the redhead's skull snapped backward.

Morrigan was too far off balance at the start of the move for the blow to be fatal, fortunately. Still, it jarred the other woman's senses, and the Angel stood and wobbled for a moment. From a prone position on her back, Morrigan blasted her with force magic and sent her flying into the cooler again.

They both got to their feet at about the same time, and Morrigan grinned. "Not so hot without your weapons?"

Her foe replied, "Bet I can say the same about you." The woman reached out, and a blizzard of cans from the nearest shelf hurtled toward Morrigan. She managed to get a force shield in place, but the impacts still knocked her sideways. The other woman closed, and Morrigan shook her head. "Enough."

She grabbed a lightning disc and slammed it down between them. Her magic deflector protected her as the electricity bit at her opponent, stunning her. She stepped in and smashed an elbow into the Angel's temple, then used her shock knuckles to blast away her consciousness when she fell to the floor. She muttered, "Jerk," then retrieved her daggers and looked for her partners.

The shapeshifter had moved immediately after landing, staying low and circling away from where she thought the bounty hunter would go. She passed behind Ruby's opponent, who writhed in the grasp of shadow tentacles coming out of her partner's arm. The sight was alarming, but it definitely seemed like a moment where restraint would be a mistake.

She spotted her foe and scuttled forward, slashing a claw at the back of her heels, intending to rip out her Achilles tendons and end the fight with a single blow. The brunette Angel must've sensed her coming because she skipped backward over the swipe. When she landed, she was about a foot away from Idryll and stepped out a kick at her face.

A backflip took the tiger-woman out of range, and her opponent lifted her rifle. Idryll charged ahead and slapped the barrel to the side, then sliced its strap away, scoring deep furrows into the woman's protective vest in the process.

Her opponent didn't waste any time trying to retain the weapon. Instead, she punched Idryll's head with her left hand and drew her pistol with her right. Idryll took the punch, which didn't have a lot of force behind it, as she stepped inside the Angel's guard and stabbed across with her claws. They penetrated the woman's forearm and caused her to drop the gun, her hand suddenly unable to function properly. Idryll twisted and whipped an elbow back at her enemy's head, but the Angel stuck her good arm in the way.

That wasn't an issue since the blow was a distraction, anyway. Idryll dipped her head forward, then stepped backward, smashing the back of her skull into the other woman's face. A muffled cry sounded in response, but the woman wrapped her damaged arm around Idryll's throat and secured the hold with her functioning hand. Her foe's muscles tensed, preparatory to crushing all the important, life-sustaining things in Idryll's neck.

An instant later, her opponent had nothing to hold onto. Idryll the house cat dashed away a few feet before returning to her humanoid form, mask and equipment belt on the floor behind her. The other woman looked completely shocked, and Idryll laughed.

"Poor girls. You had no idea what you were getting into, did you? Level one bounties? Hardly." She snapped out a kick and drove her foe back to smash into a drink cooler, a couple over from the one Morrigan had shattered with her opponent's body.

The brunette Angel made an effort to struggle out of it, but Idryll danced forward and stabbed deep into her thigh with a set of claws. The woman gasped and grabbed the wound, which had intentionally missed the big blood vessels but was at least serious enough to require immediate attention. She pointed to the side. "Medical stuff is one row over. Better take care of yourself." She turned to find the Drow for a rematch.

Ruby found herself on the wrong end of the fight. Keeping the tentacles latched on one enemy while fighting a mainly defensive battle against the Drow had resulted in a stalemate she couldn't figure out how to break. Eventually, her partners would come to her assistance, but she was afraid they'd arrive too late.

She didn't like the option of killing the bounty hunter, but it was on the table if things continued to go against her. Demetrius's voice was completely unexpected when he spoke. "PDA drone is ten seconds out, with more following."

Her opponent used her millisecond of distraction to slip a shadow blade inside her guard, slicing along her vest and cutting through to the flesh beneath. It was a shallow wound, but her attention to it allowed the bounty hunter she was trapping to writhe her way a little closer to freedom. She looked for Morrigan and Idryll, resigned to ask them for help, but they weren't in a position to intervene. She said, "Use the drone on the Drow. Quickly."

Demetrius sounded dubious but replied, "Yes." The PDA drone flew in through the open window and fired a barrage of bullets at the Drow. He dove behind the counter to safety.

Ruby used the opportunity to step forward and deliver a right hook into the bounty hunter's temple, the shock knuckles expending the last of their charges to send her into unconsciousness. By the time she got back to the Drow, Idryll was standing on the counter with an angsty expression on her face.

The shapeshifter said, "He's gone. Bastard."

Ruby sighed. "PDA troops inbound with the other drones, am I right?"

Demetrius confirmed, "Yep. Thirty seconds. Ely PD on the way, too."

She nodded and announced loudly, "If any of these wenches tries to move, shoot them with the drone. We'll let the authorities clean up this mess." Lowering her voice, she said, "Let's get out of here."

CHAPTER THIRTY

Paul Andrews stood at the head of the table and shouted, "How the hell did they penetrate our systems enough to take over a damned combat drone?"

The faces around the room displayed shock at his uncharacteristic outburst. His second in command, on the opposite side of the oval surface, replied, "We don't know how they hacked us on the cybersecurity end, but we'll find out. The good news is that we located the hardware they used for system access, and it's gone."

He shook his head. "The level of gross incompetence we're maintaining in this city has to stop. Institute checks to make sure this can't happen again."

Charlotte Krenn nodded. "Already done."

He snarled, "The rest of you, get to work. Your primary goal is to locate the damned Drow. We'll hang destroying the convenience store on him as an initial charge, and I'm sure we can whip up some more to add afterward. Alejo reached out and said she'd rounded up a few of his people, so go there and have a chat with them."

They stared at him, apparently too afraid to move, and he barked, "Dismissed. Get. Go. Charlotte, stay." They followed his orders, and a few moments later, it was only him and his most trusted subordinate. He sighed. "I'm sorry. I lost it a little there, but I also wanted to make sure everyone understood the situation."

"I get it, boss."

"What do we know right now about how they infiltrated us?"

She shrugged. "The technology was simple, a couple of signal amplifiers that gave them a route to reach our wireless system. Their infomancer is good at what he does. Since we're pretty much constantly improvising here, an opportunity existed to get the gear near ours.

"I'm still not sure how they got past our physical defenses to install the amps or how they broke through our software systems. I'm also clueless about how they figured out the location of our base, although maybe it was simply dumb luck. They seem to like rooftops."

He chuckled darkly. "That would be pretty much status quo for us here, wouldn't it?"

Krenn nodded in agreement. "Not the best gig we've ever had, that's for sure."

"So, the bounty hunters?"

"Since the bounties were gone, they were technically working outside the law. Ely PD took custody at the scene and locked them up. The Council didn't share information as to who attacked them, so they're not headed to maximum security."

He shook his head. "Too much risk there. Pull rank, have them released to us, and send them out of town to a secure facility. Once we're past all this, we'll turn them over for the attack on the Council."

She nodded. "Good call, I think."

He managed an actual laugh. "It must be hard, not saying I told you so."

She matched his smile. "Fortunately, I have a lot of practice. So, we're focusing on the Drow?"

"We are."

"And the vigilantes?"

Andrews let out a pronounced sigh. *I hate making mistakes, and going after them was apparently a big one.* "Best of luck to them. We'll take Alejo's position from here on out. So long as they don't drop any bodies and our goals remain aligned, we might as well stay out of each other's way."

Elnyier sat across from Dieneth in the bathtub built for four in her private bedroom on Oriceran. He'd been apologetic when he'd returned and seemed to think she'd be angry with him. She'd pushed him into the shower and told him to get cleaned up and join her in the tub after. Now he said, "I thought we had them."

Elnyier, who was leaning back with her eyes closed, replied calmly, "Competent enemies are always a challenge. They're also the only kind worth paying attention to."

"So you're not upset? With me, I mean?"

"Of course not. Your actions this evening will disrupt the operations of the PDA, add more fuel to the chaos swirling around Magic City, and probably set the vigilantes back on their heels. While it wasn't the great success it could have been if your plan had taken them out, it was nonetheless a step in the right direction."

Dieneth sighed, and through barely slitted eyes, she watched him recline in the bathtub as the tension flowed out of him. His feet touched her legs, and she twined them with his. He said, "I'm kind of short on people now."

Elnyier laughed. "Believe me when I say that won't be a problem. I have you covered. Our plans to increase our power in Ely will continue unabated."

Ruby had summoned everyone to the living room of the bunker to chat. Demetrius had brought a case of abbey brews, Margrave had delivered pizza and smoked salmon, and she, Morrigan, and Idryll had cleaned up and calmed down in the hours since the battle. Each of them had patched up their minor wounds and slept a little and since then had assiduously avoided talking about the previous evening's events.

When Ruby requested an update, Demetrius reported, "I've lost my connection to the PDA servers."

She nodded. "I knew that was a major risk when I told you to take over the drone. It's fine. We'll deal with it."

Morrigan asked, "Do we still have a locator on the Drow?"

Demetrius frowned. "He went to Darkest Night, and suddenly he was gone. I don't know if the locator malfunctioned, or if he threw his coat in a fire, or what."

Margrave laughed gently. "He might've portaled far

enough away that we can't track it. The locator is only good for a thirty-mile radius or so. I wouldn't call that a lost cause quite yet."

Idryll suggested, "We should break into Darkest Night and find him."

Ruby replied, "No thanks. Been there, done that, got the bruises. Besides, if he was there, we would detect him."

Her companion grumbled, "I really want to hit something."

Morrigan said, "Seconded."

Ruby nodded. "Unanimous. So moved. I'll see if Diana will let us join in a training session so we can blow off some steam."

Margrave grinned. "Pizza solves most problems, I've found."

Demetrius, around a mouthful of pizza, replied, "Seconded." Everyone laughed. After he chewed and swallowed, he said, "So, we might still have a locator on the Drow, and we don't appear to have lost any tags on the drones, either. That's all good, at least."

Morrigan asked, "What's next?"

Ruby sighed. "I don't know. I was hoping we'd get to acting instead of reacting, but that doesn't seem to have worked out so well. We've taken away the Drow's people, so that's something. I guess we'll have to wait and see what happens next and deal with it when it does."

Margrave nodded. "Wise words. It's as if being the *Mirra* of the Mist Elves has given you a new level of maturity."

Idryll added to the insult. "Don't be fooled. She's still basically a toddler with a flamethrower."

Laughter and crosstalk continued, and while everyone else seemed lighter, Ruby's thoughts grew darker. Finally, she said, "Tree, can I talk to you alone for a second?"

The others offered catcalls as she pulled him toward the receiving room, wanting to be sure she wouldn't be heard physically or magically by any of her companions. *I know he considers Shiannor a friend, so this is going to hurt a lot. But together, we'll figure out how to make it right. We'll figure out how to make it* all *right. I promise.*

Ruby's story doesn't end here. Read the epic conclusion to the Magic City Chronicles in *ALL OR NOTHING.*

THANK YOU!

Stay up to date on new releases and fan pricing by signing up for my newsletter. [CLICK HERE TO JOIN.](#)

Or visit: www.trcameron.com/Oriceran to sign up.

If you enjoyed this book, please consider leaving a review.

Thanks!

AUTHOR NOTES - TR CAMERON
JUNE 25, 2021

Thank you for reading Book 7 in the Magic City Chronicles, and for continuing on to read these author notes!

I got my patch for hiking the Fulton Trifecta! Woohoo! A great way to remember the mountain that tried to kill me. My kid was also excited about getting theirs.

Amusement park summer is on the horizon. Next week we launch into it for real with another trip to Hershey, and the week after, Six Flags in Buffalo. Mix in that with our home park, Kennywood, and there's going to be a lot of roller coasters in my near future!

I'm headed to Vegas for the 20Books show in November and will be around for the author signing event on Friday. If you're going to be around, let me know, I'd love to say hi! I will mention this on all my communication channels an endless number of times between now and then, so don't worry if you don't remember right away. I'll remind you. :D

Rogue Agents of Magic is coming along, research-wise. It'll be fun to revisit those characters as more than cameos and occasional scenes in other books. I was honestly surprised to miss them as much as I did.

I've been spending some time with audiobooks lately. *Sandman* is so worth it. I'm totally looking forward to the TV show, now, too. Also, *The Martian* has long been a favorite, and Wil Wheaton knocks the narration right out of the park. Mark Watney is partway through the long drive right now, and I've kind of forgotten how he gets from there to the end, so that will be interesting to revisit.

Season 1 of *Star Trek: Discovery* ended SO well. And now *Loki* is here. Owen Wilson is a little… odd. But really, the MCU must be running out of actors by now.

I need to say a little bit about Cruella. After the film came out, there was a whole bunch of snarky nonsense on my social media feeds commenting on how stupid the plot was. This, I'm convinced, was exclusively from people who hadn't actually seen the film. It's one part Disney, one part *Ocean's Eleven*, and one part Guy Ritchie. I am a *fan*.

Other than that, things are kind of quiet. No huge plans for the summer aside from road trips with the kid. Ani DiFranco is coming to town in September, so that's something to look forward to. I just discovered Gowan, who I liked in the 80s, is singing in place of Dennis DeYoung for Styx, who are on tour again. Somehow that seemed both notable and weird to me.

Oh! If you're not part of the Oriceran Fans Facebook group, join! There's a pizza giveaway every month, and Martha and (usually) I and all sort of fun author folks show up via Zoom to chat with our readers. It's a great time, and the community feel to it is truly fantastic. Oriceran Fans. Facebook. Your phone is probably within reach. Do it!

Before I go, once again, if this series is your first taste of my Urban Fantasy, look for "Magic Ops." I promise you'll enjoy it, and you'll get more of Diana, Rath, and company. You might also enjoy my science fiction work. All my writing is filled with action, snark, and villains who think they're heroes. Drop by www.trcameron.com and take a look!

Until next time, Joys upon joys to you and yours – so may it be.

PS: If you'd like to chat with me, here's the place. I check in daily or more: https://www.facebook.com/AuthorTRCameron. Often I put up interesting and/or silly content there, as well. For more info on my books, and to join my reader's group, please visit www.trcameron.com.

If you enjoyed this book, please consider leaving a review. Thanks!

AUTHOR NOTES - MARTHA CARR
JUNE 25, 2021

Well, what do you know? Eating right and exercising actually works, even if you're 61. I am genuinely surprised – mostly because it's me. You know, how you can believe emphatically for someone else's good fortune but for yourself – you're doomed.

That's how I've kind of felt about getting into some kind of healthy shape. I added in the word healthy because it may have taken me decades to learn this one, but dieting doesn't work. Big news flash, right?

But how many times have you listened to the ads that usually run at the beginning of the year, but post-quarantine are running now as we all emerge into the light. Puffy, doughy versions of our former selves. I've been more likely to listen to some friend who's found a book that explains everything. Keto was a favorite. I will admit that I even tried the Atkins Diet. There were two days where all I was supposed to eat was cheese. My gut locks up just thinking about it.

As a tween I even tried those candies, AIDS that were

supposed to suppress your appetite if you drank them with warm water. Glug. I ate four or five at a time and when they became associated with the name of an epidemic of the 1980's – they withered away. All for the best.

This time is different. I've stopped chasing a perfect weight that I came up with in my head based on nothing. A diet that would help me get there and then I could discard just as fast and go back to 'normal' eating. That's really been my desire all along. To look good and eat like everyone else.

That has never been my story and it only took till now for me to get it.

However, even at my age I can learn and while 'normal' is out of range, healthy is still very doable. I've cut out sugar and processed anything, baked stuff too. And I've taken up yoga and swimming again. Two forms of exercise I actually look forward to and will keep doing for longer than a year. Neither one really feels like exercise. Key for me.

And I get meditation thrown in as a bonus.

When a body gets to be 61, my current age, it was thought that the best that can be hoped for is to maintain some agility, stay in your own house and be flexible-ish. New studies, though are showing so much more is possible and quality of life can be amazing – if we can just get off the merry go round of quick fixes (which belong to the young) and focus on the bigger prize. A lifestyle that we like, can live with, and rewards us with a body that can still do just about everything. I'll let you know. I'm gonna be on this path for a while. More adventures to follow.

If you enjoyed this book, you may also enjoy the first series from T.R. Cameron, also set in the Oriceran Universe. The Federal Agents of Magic series begins with Magic Ops and it's available now at Amazon and through Kindle Unlimited.

FBI Agent Diana Sheen is an agent with a secret...

...She carries a badge and a troll, along with a little magic.

But her Most Wanted List is going to take a little extra effort.

She'll have to embrace her powers and up her game to take down new threats,

Not to mention deal with the troll that's adopted her.

All signs point to a serious threat lurking just beyond sight, pulling the strings to put the forces of good in harm's way.

Magic or mundane, you break the law, and Diana's gonna find you, tag you and bring you in. Watch out magical baddies, this agent can level the playing field.

It's all in a day's work for the newest Federal Agent of Magic.

Available now at Amazon and through Kindle Unlimited

OTHER SERIES IN THE ORICERAN UNIVERSE:

THE LEIRA CHRONICLES
SOUL STONE MAGE
THE KACY CHRONICLES
MIDWEST MAGIC CHRONICLES
THE FAIRHAVEN CHRONICLES
I FEAR NO EVIL
THE DANIEL CODEX SERIES
SCHOOL OF NECESSARY MAGIC
SCHOOL OF NECESSARY MAGIC: RAINE CAMPBELL
ALISON BROWNSTONE
FEDERAL AGENTS OF MAGIC
SCIONS OF MAGIC
THE UNBELIEVABLE MR. BROWNSTONE
DWARF BOUNTY HUNTER
CASE FILES OF AN URBAN WITCH

OTHER BOOKS BY JUDITH BERENS

OTHER BOOKS BY MARTHA CARR

OTHER SERIES IN THE ORICERAN UNIVERSE:

JOIN THE ORICERAN UNIVERSE FAN GROUP ON FACEBOOK!

BOOKS BY MICHAEL ANDERLE

Sign up for the LMBPN email list to be notified of new releases and special deals!

https://lmbpn.com/email/

For a complete list of books by Michael Anderle, please visit:

www.lmbpn.com/ma-books/

CONNECT WITH THE AUTHORS

TR Cameron Social

Website: www.trcameron.com

Facebook: https://www.facebook.com/AuthorTRCameron

Martha Carr Social

Website: http://www.marthacarr.com

Facebook: https://www.facebook.com/groups/MarthaCarrFans/

Michael Anderle Social

Website: http://lmbpn.com

Email List: http://lmbpn.com/email/

Social Media:

https://www.facebook.com/LMBPNPublishing

https://twitter.com/MichaelAnderle

https://www.instagram.com/lmbpn_publishing/

https://www.bookbub.com/authors/michael-anderle

www.ingramcontent.com/pod-product-compliance
Lightning Source LLC
LaVergne TN
LVHW041627060526
838200LV00040B/1479